animals

science

places

核心 素養
108課綱

In·Focus

英語閱讀
活用五大關鍵技巧

2

作者｜Zachary Fillingham / Owain Mckimm / Shara Dupuis

譯者｜劉嘉珮

審訂｜Richard Luhrs

MP3

寂天雲 APP

如何下載 **MP3** 音檔

❶ **寂天雲 APP 聆聽**：掃描書上 QR Code 下載
「寂天雲－英日語學習隨身聽」APP 加入會員後，
用 APP 內建掃描器再次掃描書上 QR Code，
即可使用 APP 聆聽音檔。

❷ **官網下載音檔**：請上「寂天閱讀網」
（www.icosmos.com.tw），註冊會員／登入後，
搜尋本書，進入本書頁面，點選「MP3 下載」
下載音檔，存於電腦等其他播放器聆聽使用。

Contents Chart 目錄

Introduction 簡介

　　本套書依程度共分四冊，專為初中級讀者編寫。每冊包含50篇閱讀文章、30餘種文體與題材。各冊分級主要針對文章字數多寡、字級難易度、文法深淺、句子長度來區分。生活化的主題配合多元化的體裁，讓讀者透過教材，體驗豐富多樣的語言學習經驗，提昇學習興趣，增進學習效果。

字數（每篇）	國中1200單字（每篇）	國中1201-2000單字（每篇）	高中7000(3, 4, 5級)（每篇）	文法程度	句子長度
Book 1 120–150	93%	7字	3字	（國一）first year	15字
Book 2 150–180	86%	15字	6字	（國二）second year	18字
Book 3 180–210	82%	30字	7字	（國三）third year	25字
Book 4 210–250	75%	50字	12字	（國三進階）advanced	28字

本書架構
閱讀文章

　　本套書涵蓋豐富且多元的主題與體裁。文章形式廣泛蒐羅各類生活中常見的實用體裁，包含短文、歌詞、對話、電子郵件、書序、明信片、日記、卡片、訪談等三十餘種，以日常相關的生活經驗為重點編寫設計，幫助加強基礎閱讀能力，提升基本英語溝通能力，為基礎生活英語紮根。

　　收錄大量題材有趣、多元且生活化的短文，範圍囊括青少年生活、家庭、教育、娛樂、健康、節慶、動物、藝術、文學、科學、文化、旅遊等三十餘種，主題多元化且貼近生活經驗，可激起學生學習興趣，協助學生理解不同領域知識。

閱讀測驗

每篇短文後，皆接有五題閱讀理解選擇題，評量學生對文章的理解程度。閱讀測驗所訓練學生的閱讀技巧包括：

文章中心思想
（Main Idea）／
主題（Subject Matter）

支持性細節
（Supporting Details）

從上下文猜測字義
（Words in Context）

文意推論
（Making Inferences）

看懂影像圖表
（Visualizing
Comprehension）

文章中心思想（Main Idea）

閱讀文章時，讀者可以試著問自己：「**作者想要傳達什麼訊息？**」透過審視理解的方式，檢視自己是否了解文章意義。

文章主題（Subject Matter）

這類問題幫助讀者專注在所閱讀的文章中，在閱讀文章前幾行後，讀者應該問自己：「**這篇文章是關於什麼？**」這麼做能幫助你立刻集中注意力，快速理解文章內容，進而掌握整篇文章脈絡。

支持性細節（Supporting Details）

每篇文章都是由細節組成來支持主題句。「**支持性細節**」包括範例、說明、敘述、定義、比較、對比和比喻。

從上下文猜測字義（Words in Context）

由上下文猜生字意義，是英文閱讀中一項很重要的策略。弄錯關鍵字詞的意思會導致誤解作者想要傳達的觀點。

文意推論（Making Inferences）

推論性的問題會要讀者歸納文章中已有的資訊，來思考、推理，並且將線索連結起來，推論可能的事實，這種問題的目的是訓練讀者的批判性思考和邏輯性。

看懂影像圖表（Visualizing Comprehension）

這類問題考驗讀者理解視覺資料的能力，包括表格、圖片、地圖等，或是索引、字典，學會運用這些圖像資料能增進你對文章的整體理解。

How Do I Use This Book? 使用導覽

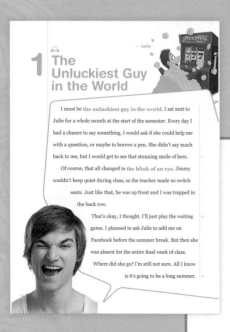

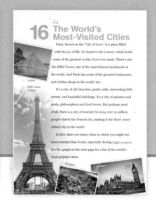

主題多元化

題材有趣且多元，貼近日常生活經驗，包含青少年生活、教育、娛樂、科學、藝術與文學等，激發學生學習興趣，協助學生理解不同領域知識。

體裁多樣化

廣納生活中常見的實用體裁，包含短文、歌詞、對話、電子郵件、書序、明信片、日記、卡片、訪談等，以日常相關生活經驗設計編寫，為基礎生活英語紮根。

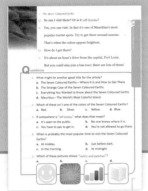

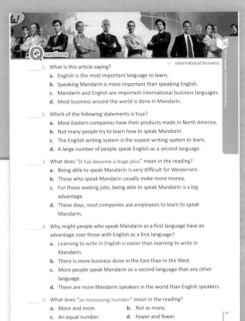

閱讀技巧練習題

左頁文章、右頁測驗的設計方式，短文後皆接有五題閱讀理解選擇題，評量學生對文章的理解程度，訓練五大閱讀技巧。

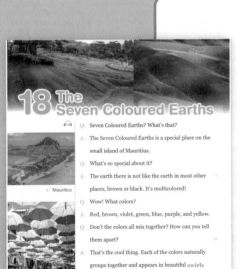

豐富多彩的圖表

運用大量彩色圖表與圖解，搭配文章輕鬆學習，以視覺輔助記憶，學習成效加倍。

1 The Unluckiest Guy in the World

» lucky

I must be **the unluckiest guy in the world**. I sat next to Julie for a whole month at the start of the semester. Every day I had a chance to say something. I would ask if she could help me with a question, or maybe to borrow a pen. She didn't say much back to me, but I would get to see that stunning smile of hers.

Of course, that all changed in **the blink of an eye**. Jimmy couldn't keep quiet during class, so the teacher made us switch seats. Just like that, he was up front and I was trapped in the back row.

That's okay, I thought. I'll just play the waiting game. I planned to ask Julie to add me on Facebook before the summer break. But then she was absent for the entire final week of class.

Where did she go? I'm still not sure. All I know is it's going to be a long summer.

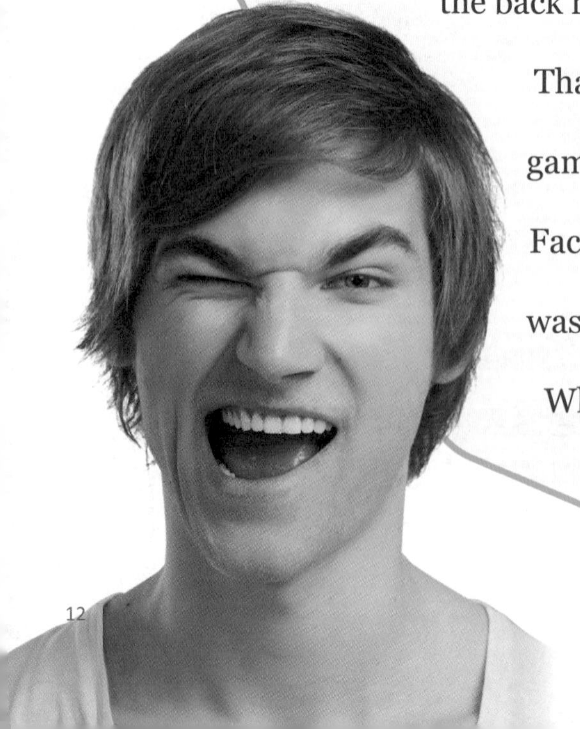

5

10

15

borrow

Questions

_____ 1. What is this reading about?

   a. A girl.   **b.** A seat.   **c.** A day.   **d.** A class.

_____ 2. Which of the following is a reason why the writer is "**the unluckiest guy in the world**"?

   a. He's at home for summer.   **b.** He switched seats in class.

   c. He uses Facebook.   **d.** He's friends with Jimmy.

_____ 3. What does "**the blink of an eye**" mean?

   a. A serious eye problem.   **b.** A season.

   c. A short amount of time.   **d.** An important exam.

_____ 4. Where does Julie sit in class?

   a. The back row.   **b.** The front row.

   c. The middle.   **d.** Beside the teacher.

_____ 5. Why was Jimmy likely moved?

   a. He couldn't hear the teacher.

   b. He liked to talk a lot.

   c. The class was too difficult for him.

   d. He was the class president.

2 Postcards From Taiwan

Dear Becky,

Taiwan is even cooler than I imagined. The people are friendly, the landscapes are beautiful, and the desserts are **to die for**.

Do you remember how I was so nervous about riding a bicycle? Well, that was silly. Lots of people ride their bikes around Taiwan. They call it a "huandao" here. The word means "around the island." There are great facilities on the road, too. It's easy to find a place to fix your bike or buy a cup of coffee. You can even spend the night in a temple **if that's your thing**.

My favorite thing about Taiwan so far is the convenience stores. This has got to be the most convenient country on Earth. There is a store on almost every corner, and they all sell these little rice triangles. They're such great snacks after a long day of riding.

I know you should be here with me and can't control what happened. But don't worry: I'll just come back with you and do it again next year!

Yours,

Linda

convenience store

rice triangles

 Chinese temple in Taiwan

⌃ Lots of people ride their bikes around Taiwan.

Questions

_____ 1. What is the main idea of this article?

   a. Taiwan has temples.
   b. Taiwan is convenient.
   c. Taiwan is great for biking.
   d. Taiwan has beautiful landscapes.

_____ 2. Which of the following is not something the writer says about Taiwan?

   a. There are convenience stores.
   b. There are places to fix your bike.
   c. The food there is cheap.
   d. Lots of people bike there.

_____ 3. What does it mean when Linda writes that Taiwan's desserts are "**to die for**"?

   a. They are dangerous.
   b. They are delicious.
   c. They are expensive.
   d. They are hard to find.

_____ 4. Which is most likely the reason Becky did not come on the trip?

   a. She thought Taiwan was too far away.
   b. She had an unexpected accident.
   c. She decided to go to Japan.
   d. She doesn't like biking.

_____ 5. What does Linda mean by saying "**if that's your thing**"?

   a. If you're scared of it.
   b. If you like doing it.
   c. If you own it.
   d. If you don't care about it.

3 School Dance

It's almost time for spring vacation, and our school is having a disco to celebrate. I'm really looking forward to it. My friend Billy is playing

5 with his band. They're really good. And some guys from the older grades are DJing, though I heard that Danny Malone has terrible taste in music. I also heard that Kenny Wallace is going.

10 He's so cute! I wonder if he'll ask me to dance . . . It's kind of embarrassing, but I'll have to ask my mom for money for the ticket. I spent all my allowance on that new top I bought at the mall last weekend. Oops!

DISCO

SCHOOL'S OU
FOR
SPRING
VACATIO

TICKETS: $.

BUY YOUR TICKET
FROM Mr. Jones
IN Classroom 25B
AT BREAKTIMES
AND LUNCH

∧ DJ (disk jockey)

« disco dance

WHEN: Friday, March 30, 6:00 p.m. – 9:00 p.m.

WHERE: The Old Gym (5th Floor, East Building)

LIVE MUSIC FROM 6:00 p.m. – 7:30 p.m.

LET'S PARTY!

FEATURING:

Billy Matthews & The History Boys

The Bright Sparks

A++

DJs From 7:30 – 9:00

DJ Danny Malone (Grade 8)

DJ Lenny Smalls (Grade 9)

Questions

1. What is the point of the poster?
   a. To tell students where the graduation party is.
   b. To give directions to the school gym.
   c. To let students know when spring vacation begins.
   d. To tell students about a school dance.

2. How much money does the writer need to borrow from her mom?
   a. Twenty dollars.
   b. Ten dollars.
   c. Five dollars.
   d. One dollar.

3. What does "A++" on the poster mean?
   a. It's the name of a band.
   b. It's the writer's school grade.
   c. It's a special VIP ticket.
   d. It's the number of a classroom.

4. What can we guess about Danny Malone?
   a. He's a great singer.
   b. He's a teacher.
   c. He's a student.
   d. He's a world-famous DJ.

5. What does the phrase "school's out" mean?
   a. School's finished.
   b. School's starting.
   c. School's cancelled.
   d. School's open.

4 Idioms to Make You Mad as a Hatter

04

Bob: What are you studying?

John: The origins and meanings of English idioms.

It's for my exam.

Bob: Oh! I'm good at these. **Try me**.

5 **John:** What does it mean when someone has his or her

"head in the clouds"?

Bob: He or she has an especially long neck, like a giraffe.

John: Not even close. It means someone is being unrealistic.

Like you are when you think Jessica will go out with you.

10 **Bob:** Very funny! Try another one.

John: What does "raining cats and dogs" mean?

Bob: That's easy. It's just a way of saying it's raining hard.

John: But do you know where it came from?

Bob: Nope.

15 **John:** There are different theories, but some say it's from when

floods used to wash up the dead bodies of cats and dogs.

Bob: Yuck. Now I have one for you.

What does it mean to be "**mad as a hatter**"?

≫ raining cats and dogs

≫ hatter

18

John: You've got me.

20 Bob: It means you're crazy. It's from when hats were made with dangerous chemicals.

John: That's how I feel when I study these idioms!

Questions

_____ 1. What is the main idea of this article?
- **a.** English has a lot of idioms.
- **b.** Idioms are an important part of language.
- **c.** Some idioms are older than others.
- **d.** English idioms can be difficult to understand.

⌃ flood

_____ 2. Which of the following is true?
- **a.** "Head in the clouds" means you're tall.
- **b.** "Raining cats and dogs" means you're unrealistic.
- **c.** Bob is studying for an exam.
- **d.** "Raining cats and dogs" has an uncertain origin.

_____ 3. What does Bob mean when he says "**try me**"?
- **a.** He wants John to ask him about idioms.
- **b.** He doesn't want to study at all.
- **c.** He thinks idioms are hard to learn.
- **d.** He is not familiar with any English idioms.

_____ 4. From the dialogue, what can we guess about the idiom "**mad as a hatter**"?
- **a.** Hat-making chemicals used to make people crazy.
- **b.** Hat makers used to earn a lot of money.
- **c.** It's one of the oldest idioms in the English language.
- **d.** Its meaning has changed a lot over the years.

_____ 5. Which of the following is probably true about Bob?
- **a.** He doesn't like John.
- **b.** He doesn't go to school.
- **c.** He likes a girl named Jessica.
- **d.** He has never seen a giraffe.

5 German Phrasebook

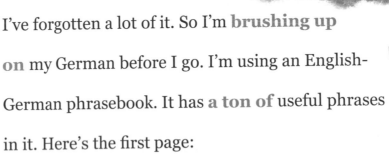

Sprechen Sie Deutsch?

I'm going to Germany on vacation next week. I studied some German in school, but I've forgotten a lot of it. So I'm **brushing up**

5   **on** my German before I go. I'm using an English-German phrasebook. It has **a ton of** useful phrases in it. Here's the first page:

Social

Basic Words and Phrases		Greetings	
Yes.	Ja.	Hello!	Hallo!
No.	Nein.	Good morning!	Guten Morgen!
Excuse me.	Entschuldigen Sie bitte.	Good afternoon!	Guten Tag!
		Good evening!	Guten Abend!
Thank you!	Danke!	Goodbye!	Auf wiedersehen!
Sorry!	Entschuldigung!		

Meeting People			
What's your name?	Wie heißt du?	Do you speak English?	Sprechen Sie Englis
My name is . . .	Ich heiße ...	I don't understand.	Das verstehe ich nicl
How are you?	Wie geht es dir?	Could you repeat that?	Bitte wiederholen.
Fine, thanks, and you?	Mir geht es gut, danke, und Ihnen?	Speak more slowly, please.	Bitte, sprechen Sie langsam.

Where is . . .? **Wo ist . . .?**

the bank	die Bank	the castle	die Burg	the museum	das Museum
the bookstore	die Buchhandlung	the hospital	das Krankenhaus	the post office	das Postamt
the bus station	der ZOB	the hotel	das Hotel	the train station	der Bahnhof

uestions

_____ 1. What is the writer's main goal in reading this book?

    a. He wants to find out about another country's culture.

    b. He wants to learn how to behave correctly.

    c. He wants to learn another language.

    d. He wants to learn where to buy the book.

_____ 2. What does the writer mean when he says he's "**brushing up on**" his German?

    a. He's reviewing something he learned before.

    b. He's studying something for the very first time.

    c. He's learning something at an advanced level.

    d. He's organizing his study schedule.

_____ 3. What does the phrase "**a ton of**" mean in the article?

    a. A piece of.   **b.** A lot of.

    c. A small amount of.   **d.** Many years of.

_____ 4. I'm in Germany, and someone asks, "**Wo ist die Burg?**" What does he or she want to know?

    a. How I am.   **b.** How to get somewhere.

    c. My name.   **d.** What language I speak.

_____ 5. I'm speaking to someone in German and he's talking too fast. What should I say?

    a. Auf Wiedersehen!   **b.** Mir geht es gut, danke, und Ihnen?

    c. Wie geht es dir?   **d.** Bitte, sprechen Sie langsam.

6 When to Reach for a Glass of Water

By now, everyone knows that drinking water is good for our health. Many of us already drink the eight glasses (2000 cc) a day we're told to. But did you know it makes a big difference when you drink them? Here are the best times to reach for a glass:

1) **After you wake up:** two glasses of water in the morning will help start up your internal organs and clean your blood.

2) **Before a meal:** have a glass 30 minutes before you eat. This has two important benefits. It will help you avoid eating too much. It will also help your body absorb the food.

3) **Before a bath:** a glass of water before a bath can help lower your blood pressure.

4) **Before and after exercise:** it's important that your body has enough water when you exercise. **This** will also benefit your liver.

5) **Before bed:** a glass of water before bed will improve your heart's health.

>> Drink water after you wake up.

22

« Drink water before eating.

⌃ Drink water before taking a bath.

⌃ Drink water before and after exercise.

⌃ Drink water before you go to sleep.

Questions

_____ 1. What's the main idea of this article?

    a. Water is good for your health.

    b. You should drink water at certain times.

    c. Always drink water before a bath.

    d. Water can help clean your blood.

_____ 2. Which of the following is not a good time to drink water according to the article?

    a. Before bed.   **b.** After waking up.

    c. Before going to work.   **d.** Before and after exercise.

_____ 3. What does "**This**" mean?

    a. Getting a lot of exercise.   **b.** Drinking water before exercise.

    c. Eating less.   **d.** Drinking water before a bath.

_____ 4. Which of the following is likely true?

    a. Drinking water can cause high blood pressure.

    b. People who shower shouldn't drink water.

    c. Doctors say to drink eight glasses of water a day.

    d. You should never drink water after a meal.

_____ 5. Which of the following is likely true about exercise?

    a. It damages the liver.   **b.** It activates your internal organs.

    c. It uses up water.   **d.** It should only be done at night.

↟ smartphones

7 07
What's Your Favorite Class?

Chris

John

C Today's math class was like **watching paint dry**.

LOL. Aren't they all a bit dull? **J**

C No way! Some classes are great. I look forward to English class because it helps me understand my favorite shows. 5

I guess I do enjoy history class sometimes. **J**

C What do you like about **it**? 10

I like thinking about how the world was before smartphones, computers, and even television. Life was so different 100 years ago. 15 **J**

« modern computer gadgets

⩔ television

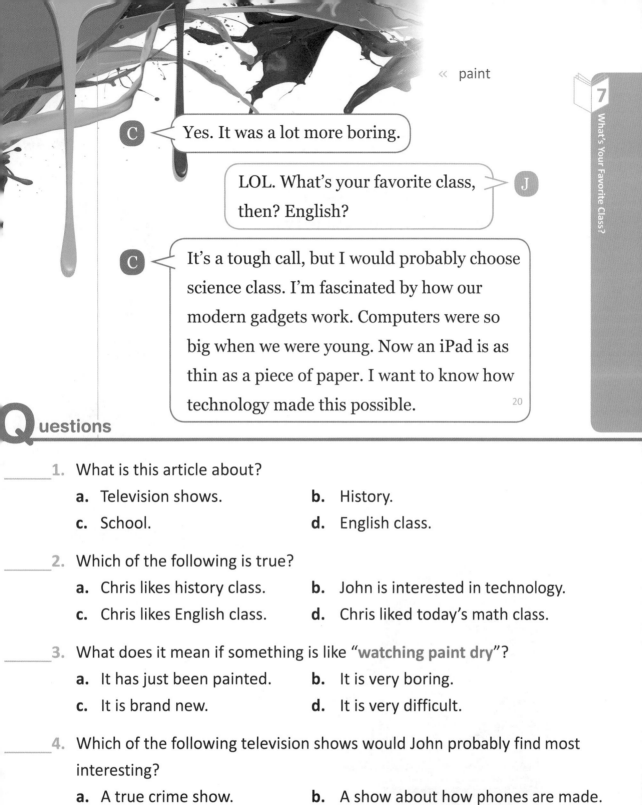

C Yes. It was a lot more boring.

J LOL. What's your favorite class, then? English?

C It's a tough call, but I would probably choose science class. I'm fascinated by how our modern gadgets work. Computers were so big when we were young. Now an iPad is as thin as a piece of paper. I want to know how technology made this possible. ²⁰

Questions

1. What is this article about?
   a. Television shows.　　b. History.
   c. School.　　d. English class.

2. Which of the following is true?
   a. Chris likes history class.　b. John is interested in technology.
   c. Chris likes English class.　d. Chris liked today's math class.

3. What does it mean if something is like "watching paint dry"?
   a. It has just been painted.　b. It is very boring.
   c. It is brand new.　d. It is very difficult.

4. Which of the following television shows would John probably find most interesting?
   a. A true crime show.　b. A show about how phones are made.
   c. A news show.　d. A drama about ancient China.

5. What does "it" mean?
   a. History class.　　b. A smartphone.
   c. English class.　　d. Paint.

8 Greetings From Home

My dear Cindy, I just wanted you to know how proud we all are. It seems like just yesterday you went to go study overseas. I can't believe that was four

5   years ago. Congratulations and we're all thinking of you, even Mittens. I gave him a big bone to celebrate the event.

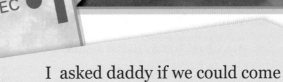

I asked daddy if we could come and see your big day. He said it would be too expensive. Good thing you're coming home in a few months, anyway!

Don't forget to bring back presents. Mom says that Germany has the best gummy bears in the world.

REC

00.05.39.11

I remember when you first told me you wanted to be a scientist. That was about ten years ago, and now you're making your dream come true. Please make sure that someone takes a few pictures of the ceremony. Remember to show everyone your wonderful smile. And most important of all: enjoy your **moment in the spotlight**. You've earned it!

20

Questions

_____ 1. What are the people in this video trying to say?
- **a.** It's okay to make mistakes.
- **b.** Great job.
- **c.** It's important to travel.
- **d.** False alarm.

_____ 2. How long has Cindy been away?
- **a.** A few days.
- **b.** Ten years.
- **c.** A few months.
- **d.** Four years.

_____ 3. What would be another example of a "**moment in the spotlight**"?
- **a.** Giving a speech.
- **b.** Going shopping.
- **c.** Watching a movie.
- **d.** Lining up.

_____ 4. What are the people likely helping Cindy to celebrate?
- **a.** Her wedding.
- **b.** Her birthday.
- **c.** Finishing school.
- **d.** Opening a store.

_____ 5. Who is Mittens?
- **a.** Cindy's brother.
- **b.** Cindy's cousin.
- **c.** The family dog.
- **d.** The family cat.

9 Better to Be Yourself Than Perfect

It's okay not to be perfect.

It sounds strange, right? That's because we're used to trying to be perfect. Our parents want us to get full marks. We want the very best in life. And our minds never stop looking for new
5 ways to improve.

But here's the **catch**. Although it's good to have goals, you're more likely to achieve them by just being yourself. Trying to be perfect only makes things more difficult. It adds stress and slows you down by making you overthink everything. It's better
10 to just calmly and coolly get the job done. Even if you make a mistake, you can learn from it next time.

Remember that perfection doesn't even actually exist. It's just an idea that we have fallen in love with. Even if you did achieve "perfection," you wouldn't know it. You'd be too busy
15 worrying about how to improve on **it**.

Questions

1. What is this article trying to say?

   a. Always be perfect.
   b. Listen to your parents.
   c. Be brave and be yourself.
   d. It's good to have goals.

2. Which of the following is not a tip from the article?

   a. Slow down when you're feeling stressed.
   b. Be yourself.
   c. Learn from mistakes.
   d. Always get full marks.

3. Which of the following sentences uses "**catch**" in the same way as the article?

   a. The baseball player made a great catch.
   b. Use the catch to close the window.
   c. The fisherman returned with a big catch.
   d. There was a catch in the agreement.

4. Which of the following tips would the writer likely offer?

   a. Don't be scared to make mistakes.
   b. The faster you do something, the better.
   c. You should learn to love perfection.
   d. Worry about what others think of you.

5. What is "**it**"?

   a. Love.
   b. Perfection.
   c. A catch.
   d. A mistake.

« stress

aim for PROGRESS not PERFECTION

⌃ Perfection doesn't exist.

10 Welcome to the Sunnyside Dog Park!

To enjoy the dog park fully, please pay close attention to the following rules.

 Do remove your dog's collar on entering the park. Collars get caught on fences and can cause injuries or choking.

 Do clean up after your dog. We want the dog park to be a clean environment for both dogs and people to play in!

 Do exercise your dog well before entering the dog park. Though the park is a great place for dogs to **let off some steam** dogs with too much energy to start with often cause trouble!

Questions

_____ 1. What can you learn from the notice?
- **a.** What time is best to visit the dog park.
- **b.** How much you have to pay to use the dog park.
- **c.** How to behave in the dog park.
- **d.** Why it's good to take your dog to the dog park.

_____ 2. Which of the following should you do before entering the dog park?
- **a.** Wash your dog.
- **b.** Feed your dog.
- **c.** Put a collar on your dog.
- **d.** Exercise your dog.

⌃ dog park

⌃ dog tag

⌃ dog collar

Do keep your small dog in the small dog section. Small dogs who ¹⁰ play with big dogs often get hurt!

Don't bring your child to the dog park. There are a lot of big dogs running around. This can sometimes be dangerous for little kids.

Don't feed anyone else's dog without the owner's permission. Some dogs have food allergies. It can be dangerous to feed them. ¹⁵

Don't bring your dog to the park if he or she is sick. He or she might pass **it** on to other dogs.

We hope you and your dog have fun!

_____ 3. What do you do if you "**let off some steam**"?

    a. Store energy for later.   **b.** Use your last bit of energy.

    c. Use up extra energy.   **d.** Get more energy.

_____ 4. Which of these can we guess about the dog park?

    a. Dogs of all sizes are welcome.

    b. Only big dogs are allowed.

    c. The park is not safe for small dogs.

    d. Only medium-sized dogs can use the park.

_____ 5. What is "**it**"?

    a. Your dog.   **b.** Sickness.   **c.** The park.   **d.** Food.

11

A Most Delicious Debate: Who Invented the Hamburger?

Mark: And for the last stop on our trip, we visited the birthplace of the hamburger.

Klaus: Hold on a second. The hamburger was invented in Germany.

5 **Mark:** I think you're mistaken. It was invented in the United States. Hamburgers are "American as apple pie," as we say back home. For proof you need **look no further** than McDonald's.

Klaus: Rubbish! Every German knows that hamburgers
10 come from Hamburg. The proof lies in how the word is spelled.

Waitress: Excuse me, gentlemen, but I couldn't help overhearing your argument. I'm a bit of a foodie, and I
15 happen to know a lot about hamburgers.

» foodie

20

In a way you're both right. The ground meat part came from Germany. The bun, on the other hand, was an American invention. It was added because factory workers had to eat their "Hamburg steaks" quickly and get back to work.

Klaus: Well, the meat is the most important part.

Mark: What? The bun is what makes a hamburger.

Waitress: Oh, dear . . .

Questions

⌃ Hamburg, Gemany

1. What is the main idea of this article?
   a. Hamburgers are delicious.
   b. McDonald's serves the best hamburgers.
   c. Hamburgers have a long history.
   d. Klaus and Mark are friends.

2. Why was a bun added to the hamburger?
   a. To make it taste better.   b. To let people eat it faster.
   c. To make it more expensive.   d. To put on more ketchup.

3. What does the writer mean by saying "look no further"?
   a. This is what you're looking for.   b. This is something that's missing.
   c. This is worth arguing over.   d. This is a funny joke.

4. Which of the following is probably true about Mark?
   a. He hates hamburgers.   b. He's American.
   c. He works at McDonald's.   d. He just met Klaus.

5. Where is the conversation likely taking place?
   a. A school.   b. An office.   c. A bus.   d. A restaurant.

12 Olympic Games All-Time Medal Wins

I love sport, so naturally I'm really looking forward to the next Olympics. I'm from Great Britain, and although **we** never win the most medals, we always win our fair share. The country that almost always beats everyone else in the medals table, though, is the United States.

5   In fact, the United States has won more gold and overall medals than any other country in the Summer Games. It's number one on the chart on the next page, see? It's won a total of 2,552 medals, including 1,018 gold medals, since the modern Olympic Games began in 1896. Even I have to say, that's pretty amazing.

Questions

_____ 1. The countries are listed on the chart for their successes in which field?

   a. Sport.   **b.** Music.   **c.** Health.   **d.** Science.

_____ 2. Which of the following is true according to the writer?

   a. The United States never wins the most medals.

   b. Great Britain always wins the most medals.

   c. The United States usually wins the most medals.

   d. Great Britain never wins a medal.

_____ 3. Who are "**we**" in the second sentence?

   a. The writer.   **b.** Great Britain.

   c. The Olympic Games.   **d.** Gold medals.

« bronze medal

« silver medal

« gold medal

All-Time Summer Medal Standings, 1896–2012

Rank	Nation	Gold	Silver	Bronze	Total
1	United States of America	1,018	824	710	2,552
2	USSR	473	376	355	1,204
3	Germany	232	235	251	718
4	Italy	227	189	211	627
5	Great Britain	217	258	262	737
6	France	217	239	273	729
7	Democratic Republic of Germany	192	165	162	519
8	Sweden	190	192	222	604
9	China	172	135	122	429
10	Norway	161	154	133	448

_____ 4. According to the chart, how many gold medals did Norway win between 1896 and 2012?

   a. One hundred fifty-four.

   b. Four hundred forty-eight.

   c. One hundred thirty-three.

   d. One hundred sixty-one.

_____ 5. Which of the following is true?

   a. Italy has won more medals overall than Great Britain.

   b. Italy has won more gold medals than Great Britain.

   c. Italy has won more silver medals than Great Britain.

   d. Italy has won more bronze medals than Great Britain.

Will you ever fall in love?

Who were you in a past life?

When will you have children?

*Does he or she like you as **more than a friend?***

Will you ever find your soul mate?

If you have questions about your past, present, or future,

Madam Clara

has the answers.

"Before I met with Madam Clara, I worried that I would never get married. She told me I would get married within the next year. Now, I can finally stop worrying and be positive about my future!"

~Stephanie, age 34

"Madam Clara told me that I wasn't getting a promotion at work because I lacked confidence. Now, I'm an assistant manager in a large company."

~David, age 42

"I've always liked learning about biology but didn't know why. Madam Clara told me that I was a scientist in a previous life!"

~Jessica, age 25

"I was worried about passing a test. Madam Clara told me that as long as I studied, I would succeed—and I did!"

~Stan, age 16

Call Madam Clara today!
897-432-9890

≫ fortune-teller ≫ job promotion ≫ scientist

Questions

_____ 1. What is the reading mainly about?
- **a.** Madam Clara is great at her job.
- **b.** Most people worry about their futures.
- **c.** It is expensive to have your fortune told.
- **d.** Madam Clara can help you find love.

_____ 2. What does "**more than a friend**" mean in the reading?
- **a.** In a superficial way.
- **b.** Like a best friend.
- **c.** In a romantic way.
- **d.** Like a family member.

_____ 3. How did David become a manager?
- **a.** Madam Clara arranged a promotion.
- **b.** He stopped worrying so much.
- **c.** Madam Clara helped him find love.
- **d.** He improved his confidence.

_____ 4. Why has Stephanie stopped worrying?
- **a.** Because she got married.
- **b.** Madam Clara helped her start a new friendship.
- **c.** She's decided she doesn't want to get married.
- **d.** Because she knows she will meet someone soon.

_____ 5. Whose past life did Madam Clara read?
- **a.** David's.
- **b.** Stephanie's.
- **c.** Jessica's.
- **d.** Stan's.

14

» Robots will soon replace blue-collar workers.

Will Robots Help Us or Just Steal Our Jobs?

Humans have dreamed of robots doing our work for hundreds of years. However, now that **it**'s happening, it may turn out to be more of a nightmare.

5 The idea works in theory: robots doing all the work so we have more time to relax. But in practice it's totally different. When a robot replaces a human worker, that worker simply loses his or her job. There's no time to kick back and relax, just a frantic search for a new job. And you had better find one the robots can't do—yet.

10 Human workers will soon be replaced on a large scale. One study says that 45% of jobs in the United States will be done by robots by 2030. Robots may soon be working as nurses, teachers, clerks, cleaners, and even writers. In fact, computers have already **taken over** the writing of some news articles.

15 Perhaps even this article was written by a robot!

_____ 1. What is the main idea of this article?

   a. Robots are dangerous.   **b.** The robots are coming.

   c. Robots can teach children.   **d.** Humans are better than robots.

_____ 2. According to the article, which of the following statements is not true?

   a. Computers are already writing some articles.

   b. There are already robot nurses.

   c. A study says 45% of US work will be done by robots by 2030.

   d. Humans have dreamed of robot workers for centuries.

_____ 3. What does it mean when the writer says that computers have "**taken over**" writing news articles?

   a. They have taken control of the job from humans.

   b. They have helped humans do the job.

   c. They have tried to do the job but have failed.

   d. They have fought with humans for the job.

_____ 4. Which is likely not a reason why robots are replacing human workers?

   a. They are cheaper.   **b.** They are faster.

   c. They work longer.   **d.** They need power.

_____ 5. What is "**it**"?

   a. A worker.   **b.** The dream of robot workers.

   c. A job.   **d.** The nightmare of robot workers.

Robots will continue their migration into white-collar work.

The Amazing Max

His name is known far and wide,

To humans and dogs alike.

His name is known far and wide,

As a pet who will fight for what's right.　　　5

Max! They whisper, he cannot be caught,

And digs up five flower beds a day.

Max! They say, he's faster than fast,

And will make all the mailmen pay.

Questions

_____ 1. What is the main idea of this song?
- **a.** Max is a naughty dog.
- **b.** Max digs up flower beds.
- **c.** Max is very talented.
- **d.** Max is fast.

_____ 2. Which of the following is not true about Max?
- **a.** He escaped from the pound.
- **b.** He helps people cross the street.
- **c.** He likes to chase mailmen.
- **d.** He only goes out at night.

_____ 3. What does "some" refer to in the first line of the third verse?
- **a.** People who don't like dogs.
- **b.** People who own dogs.
- **c.** People who help the blind.
- **d.** People who enjoy gardening.

Try though they might, **some** just can't accept, 10

That a dog could rise high in regard.

What, they ask, could be so great,

About a fleabag tied up in the yard?

Well, just ask the old man who works at the pound,

Who discovered his empty cage. 15

Or the blind woman he helped to cross the street,

For but a tummy rub in exchange.

Max! They'll say, that dog is amazing,

I wish he would settle down and stay.

Max! They'll say, is living proof,

That **every dog has his day**.

» tummy rub

_____4. Which of the following is probably true about Max?
  a. He's scared of people.   **b.** He is always moving around.
  c. He sleeps out in the yard.   **d.** He is owned by a mailman.

_____5. What does the phrase "**every dog has his day**" mean in the song?
  a. Everyone gets a chance to shine.
  b. Even dogs have birthdays.
  c. Having pets is a lot of hard work.
  d. It's hard to become famous.

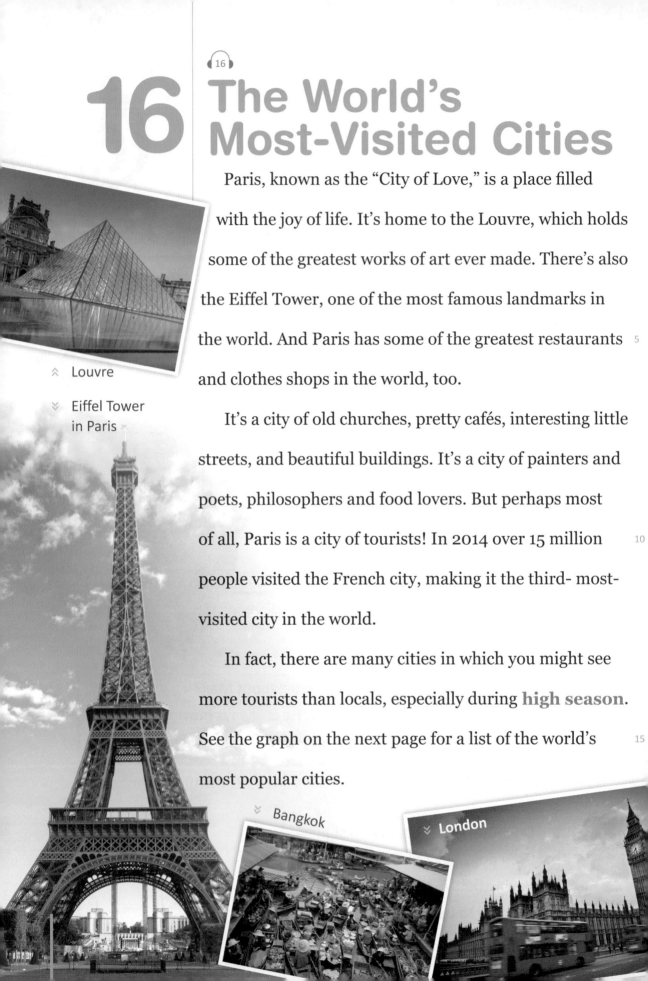

16 The World's Most-Visited Cities

Paris, known as the "City of Love," is a place filled with the joy of life. It's home to the Louvre, which holds some of the greatest works of art ever made. There's also the Eiffel Tower, one of the most famous landmarks in the world. And Paris has some of the greatest restaurants 5 and clothes shops in the world, too.

It's a city of old churches, pretty cafés, interesting little streets, and beautiful buildings. It's a city of painters and poets, philosophers and food lovers. But perhaps most of all, Paris is a city of tourists! In 2014 over 15 million 10 people visited the French city, making it the third- most-visited city in the world.

In fact, there are many cities in which you might see more tourists than locals, especially during **high season**. See the graph on the next page for a list of the world's 15 most popular cities.

⌃ Louvre

⌄ Eiffel Tower in Paris

⌄ Bangkok

⌄ London

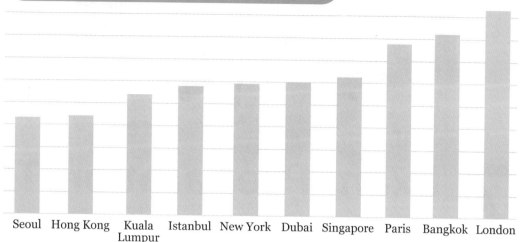

Most-Visited Cities of 2014

Number of Visitors (Millions)

Seoul | Hong Kong | Kuala Lumpur | Istanbul | New York | Dubai | Singapore | Paris | Bangkok | London

Questions

_____ 1. Why did the writer write about Paris in this article?

    a. It has many art museums.

    b. It's a very popular tourist spot.

    c. It has world-class food.

    d. It has beautiful buildings.

_____ 2. Which of the following was true about Paris in 2014?

    a. It got over 20 million visitors.

    b. It was the most-visited city in the world.

    c. Two cities got more visitors than it did.

    d. More people visited New York.

_____ 3. Which of the following most likely happens during "**high season**"?

    a. Most hotels become fully booked.

    b. People throw out their old clothes.

    c. The weather becomes cold and wet.

    d. Shops close earlier than usual.

_____ 4. What was the most-visited city of 2014?

    a. Seoul.   **b.** Bangkok.   **c.** London.   **d.** New York.

_____ 5. How many visitors did Hong Kong get in 2014?

    a. Seven and a half million.   **b.** Ten million.

    c. Just over 11 million.   **d.** Almost nine million.

17 Exam Preparation Tips

Studying for an exam can be extremely stressful. No matter how ready you are, there's always a risk that something bad could happen on exam day. Maybe you get surprised by a question, or you lose your cool and write a bad answer.

5 Luckily, there are ways to make sure **this** doesn't happen. It just takes a careful and organized approach to exam preparation. Here are a few important tips to help you succeed:

Questions

_____ 1. What is this article trying to say?
- **a.** There are ways to improve your studying.
- **b.** Studying for exams is very hard.
- **c.** There's a risk something could happen on exam day.
- **d.** Always study in a clean and quiet area.

_____ 2. Which of the following is not a study tip from the article?
- **a.** Use pictures to study.
- **b.** Study in a quiet area.
- **c.** Practice on old exams.
- **d.** Always study alone.

_____ 3. What does it mean to "**get the hang**" of something?
- **a.** To fully understand it.
- **b.** To say it out loud.
- **c.** To discuss it with a friend.
- **d.** To forget it.

- Practice on old exams to **get the hang** of the subject matter.

10 - Arrange study groups with your classmates to get their points of view.

☆ study group

- Eat foods that support your memory, like fish, fruits, and nuts.

- Use visual tools to study, like charts and

15 pictures.

☆ visual tools

- Don't always study in the same place.

- Study in a clean and quiet area.

- Take short breaks to give your mind a rest.

- Plan out your exam day so there are no

20 surprises on the way to school.

☆ Study in a clean and quiet area.

_____ **4.** Which would likely be another study tip from the writer?
- **a.** Study in front of the television.
- **b.** Cheat on the exam if you're not well prepared.
- **c.** Get a good sleep the night before the exam.
- **d.** Drink lots of cola before taking the exam.

_____ **5.** What is "**this**"?
- **a.** Something bad happening on exam day.
- **b.** An exam making you laugh.
- **c.** Being careful about an exam.
- **d.** A new way to prepare for your exams.

18 The Seven Coloured Earths

≫ Mauritius

≫ Port Louis, Mauritius

Q: Seven Coloured Earths? What's that?

A: The Seven Coloured Earths is a special place on the small island of Mauritius.

Q: What's so special about it?

A: The earth there is not like the earth in most other places, brown or black. It's multicolored!

Q: Wow! What colors?

A: Red, brown, violet, green, blue, purple, and yellow.

Q: Don't the colors all mix together? How can you tell them apart?

A: That's the cool thing. Each of the colors naturally groups together and appears in beautiful **swirls and patches**. It's quite a sight!

Q: How does that happen?

A: You know what? Nobody really knows! Also, the earth never wears away, even though the area gets some very heavy rain. Strange, right?

Q: So can I visit there? Or is it **off limits**?

A: Yes, you can visit. In fact it's one of Mauritius's most

popular tourist spots. Try to get there around sunrise. 20

That's when the colors appear brightest.

Q: How do I get there?

A: It's about an hour's drive from the capital, Port Louis.

But you could also join a bus tour; there are lots of them!

Questions

_____ 1. What might be another good title for the article?
   a. The Seven Coloured Earths—Where It Is and How to Get There
   b. The Strange Case of the Seven Coloured Earths
   c. Everything You Wanted to Know about the Seven Coloured Earths
   d. Mauritius—The World's Most Colorful Island

_____ 2. Which of these isn't one of the colors of the Seven Coloured Earths?
   a. Red.   **b.** Silver.   **c.** Yellow.   **d.** Blue.

_____ 3. If somewhere is "**off limits**," what does that mean?
   a. It's open to the public.   **b.** No one knows where it is.
   c. You have to pay to get in.   **d.** You're not allowed to go there.

_____ 4. When is probably the most popular time to visit the Seven Coloured Earths?
   a. At midday.   **b.** Just before dark.
   c. In the morning.   **d.** At midnight.

_____ 5. Which of these pictures shows "**swirls and patches**"?
   a.   **b.**   **c.**   **d.**

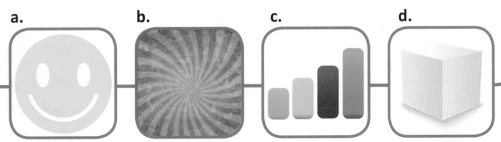

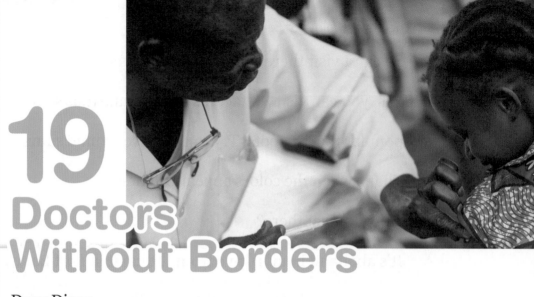

19
Doctors Without Borders

Dear Diary,

I was **drawn to** Doctors Without Borders because I wanted to help people. Its members go into any country where they're needed. There's no politics, just the question of helping those in need. As a

5　doctor I had useful skills, so I decided to join up.

Back then I thought I would be giving children shots in Albania or some small African village. I had no idea that I would be on the front lines of a "**hot zone.**" We have been in Liberia for a year, and it seems we're finally winning the fight against Ebola. However, I still

10　have to follow all the rules. Before entering the hospital, I put on four layers of plastic. It can get very hot under there, but I can't touch my face. That would be too dangerous.

There are doctors and nurses from all around the world here, but we all agree on one thing. This is

15　a hard job, but someone has to

do it.

>> The Ebola virus is a fatal illness.

« Doctors Without Borders outpost in Darfur (2005)

⌄ Doctors Without Borders is a humanitarian aid organization.

MEDECINS SANS FRONTIERES
DOCTORS WITHOUT BORDERS

Questions

1. What is this article about?

   a. A doctor.

   b. Ebola.

   c. An organization.

   d. An African village.

⌃ Albanian refugees line up for care at a Doctors Without Borders medical center.

2. Where was the writer sent by Doctors Without Borders?

   a. Albania.
   b. A small African village.

   c. Liberia.
   d. All around the world.

3. What does "**drawn to**" mean in the article?

   a. To be afraid of something.
   b. To be far away from something.

   c. To cure something.
   d. To be very interested in something.

4. Which is likely another example of a "**hot zone**"?

   a. An island with very humid weather.

   b. A village with a very dangerous flu.

   c. A village with lots of children in need of shots.

   d. A city with lots of poor people in need.

5. Which of the following statements is likely true about Doctors Without Borders?

   a. It doesn't accept women.
   b. It operates in many countries.

   c. All doctors must join it.
   d. It only operates in "hot zones."

» *Pirates of the Caribbean: On Stranger Tides* is the most expensive film ever made.

20

Movie Budget Breakdown

Movies cost a lot of money to make. The most expensive film ever made to date (*Pirates of the Caribbean: On Stranger Tides*, 2011) cost over $378 million. Movie studios are usually quite secretive about how much they spend and what they spend it on. So, often we don't know

5 exactly how much a studio spends on, **say**, special effects or music. It's safe to say, though, that it changes with each movie.

Questions

_____ 1. What does the pie chart show about the movie *Unbreakable*?
   a. How much money it made.   **b.** How much time it took to make.
   c. How much it cost to make.   **d.** How many people worked on it.

_____ 2. Look at how much money was spent on special effects compared to actors. What can we guess about *Unbreakable* from this?
   a. The movie is a drama.   **b.** The movie has no special effects.
   c. The movie got bad reviews.   **d.** The movie is not okay for children

_____ 3. What does the word "**say**" mean in the sentence " . . . we don't know exactly how much a studio spends on, **say**, special effects or music"?
   a. However.   **b.** In addition.
   c. For example.   **d.** As a result.

Each movie is different. Some are big science fiction pictures, which take place in space or have lots of crazy-looking monsters. These movies will probably spend large parts of their budgets on special effects. Other types of movies, like dramas, will have much smaller budgets and will spend much more on the actors than on special effects. Here you can see the budget breakdown for the movie *Unbreakable*, starring Bruce Willis. It had a total budget of $74,243,106.

Unbreakable Budget Breakdown

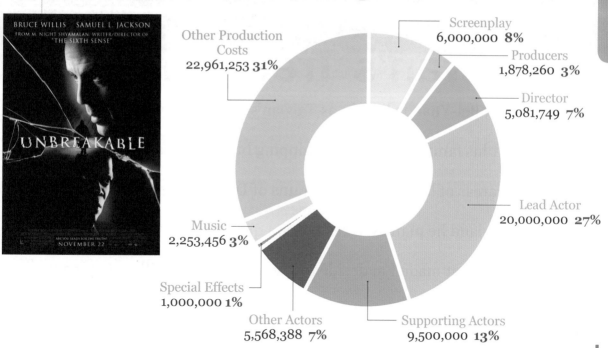

Other Production Costs
22,961,253 **31%**

Screenplay
6,000,000 **8%**

Producers
1,878,260 **3%**

Director
5,081,749 **7%**

Lead Actor
20,000,000 **27%**

Music
2,253,456 **3%**

Special Effects
1,000,000 **1%**

Other Actors
5,568,388 **7%**

Supporting Actors
9,500,000 **13%**

_____ 4. Bruce Willis was the lead actor in the movie *Unbreakable*.
How much did he get paid?

   a. Twenty million dollars.   **b.** Nine and a half million dollars.

   c. Five million dollars.   **d.** Seventy four million dollars.

_____ 5. About how much of the movie's budget was spent on music?

   a. Thirteen percent.   **b.** Thirty-one percent.

   c. Seven percent.   **d.** Three percent.

» Lai, Bei-Yuan

21
Taiwan's Tree King

Lai, Bei-Yuan is known as Taiwan's Tree King. Over 30 years ago he left his family's successful shipping business and began buying large areas of land in the mountains of Dasyueshan in Taichung. And on this land he planted trees—over a quarter of a million of them!

5   But what made Lai decide to spend over NT$2 billion buying land to plant trees? Lai says that the customers he used to serve as part of his day job were all in businesses that polluted the earth. He felt that he needed to do something to **restore** the earth's life energy.

The trees Lai plants are all types that can grow for a thousand

10   years or more! **They** help hold the soil together and keep water flowing through the earth.

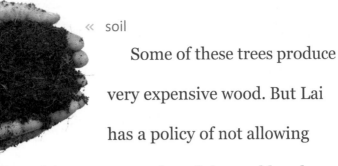

« soil

Some of these trees produce very expensive wood. But Lai has a policy of not allowing

15 anyone to cut down his trees, even though he could make a lot of money from it.

　　As long as the Tree King is around, his forest will be safe.

» planting trees

Questions

_____ 1. This article is about a man named Lai, Bei-Yuan. Which part of his life does it focus on?

    a. His childhood.　**b.** His work with the environment.

    c. His children.　**d.** His family shipping business.

_____ 2. How many trees has Lai planted?

    a. Over 250,000.　　　　**b.** Over 2,000,000,000.

    c. About 30.　　　　　　**d.** Just over 1,000.

_____ 3. What does "**restore**" most likely mean?

    a. Bring back.　**b.** Take away.　**c.** Cut down.　**d.** Buy up.

_____ 4. Why doesn't Lai let anyone cut down his trees?

    a. He wants to cut them down himself.

    b. He wants to wait until the price of wood goes up.

    c. He needs them to protect his house from rain.

    d. His beliefs are more important to him than money.

_____ 5. Who or what are "**they**"?

    a. Lai and his family.　　**b.** Businesses.

    c. Trees.　　　　　　　　**d.** Customers.

22 Breaking Up Is Hard to Do

⌃ cheat

⌃ Sometimes you lose self-confidence after a breakup.

Jill Brown is the host of a popular television show. Today she is interviewing Sarah Thompson, a relationship expert who recently published a book.

Jill: Could you tell us a little about your book?

5 Sarah: **It** talks about what I believe to be a very important subject: breaking up.

Jill: That's something many of us have experienced before. Could you tell us a bit more?

Sarah: The book **pulls no punches** on what it feels like

10 to break up with someone you love: It's the worst feeling in the world. You second-guess yourself, wonder if you can love again, and lose all your self-confidence. Sometimes it can seem like the world is ending.

15 Jill: How can someone get through this awful period?

Sarah: Remember that these feelings are temporary. Although it might be painful now, things will improve with time. In a year or two you'll look back on the breakup with totally new eyes. Therefore the key thing is never to hurt yourself or anyone else.

Jill: Well said. I wish your book had been there when I was a teenager.

20

Questions

_____ 1. What is this article about?

     a. A book.   **b.** A breakup.   **c.** A host.   **d.** An argument.

_____ 2. Which of the following is not one of Sarah's points on breakups?

     a. It can feel like the world is ending.

     b. You can lose confidence in yourself.

     c. The bad feelings never go away.

     d. Never hurt yourself or others.

_____ 3. What does it mean that Sarah's book "**pulls no punches**"?

     a. It discusses fighting.   **b.** It tells the whole truth.

     c. It discusses a sad subject.   **d.** It was recently published.

_____ 4. Which of the following is probably true about Jill?

     a. She hosts several different shows.

     b. She had a bad breakup when she was younger.

     c. She doesn't like Sarah's book very much.

     d. She doesn't think breaking up with someone is a big deal.

_____ 5. What is "**it**"?

     a. How it feels to break up.   **b.** Jill's television show.

     c. Loving someone.   **d.** Sarah's new book.

23. Using the Metro

» The New York City Subway is the system with the most stations.

Subways (also called metro systems or undergrounds) are a vital part of modern cities. They allow millions of passengers to get to where they need to go each day quickly and cheaply.

Currently, there are more than 160 subway systems in operation
5 worldwide. The largest metro system is the Shanghai Metro, which has a total route length of almost 550 km. The system with the most stations, however, is the New York City Subway. It has a total of 421 stations!

To find your way around a metro system, use a metro map. The lines are **color coded**. And the stations are all marked and named. You'll
10 notice that some stations have two lines running through them. These are "transfer stations," where you can change from one line to another without having to exit the
15 metro system.

Here's an example of a typical metro map. Do you think you could use it to get around the city?

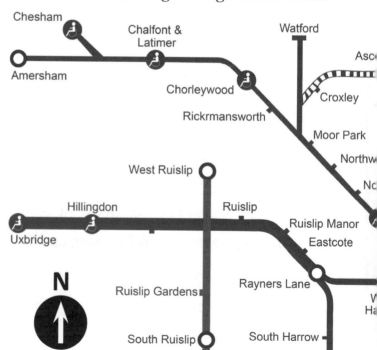

Questions

_____ 1. What does the map do?

    a. It shows you how to get around a city on public transport.

    b. It shows you the quickest way to drive through a city.

    c. It shows you how to find a certain building in a city.

    d. It shows how to do a tour of a city on foot.

_____ 2. What does the writer say about metro systems?

    a. There are over 200 in the world.

    b. No one uses them very much.

    c. They're very cheap to build.

    d. People who live in cities really need them.

_____ 3. What does the writer mean by saying that the metro lines are "**color coded**"?

    a. They're difficult to understand.   **b.** They're all very long.

    c. They're easy to tell apart.   **d.** They're not complete.

_____ 4. I'm at Rayners Lane Station. I want to get to Ruislip Station. What should I do?

    a. Take the blue line towards Uxbridge.

    b. Take the red line towards Amersham.

    c. Take the orange line towards West Ruislip.

    d. Take the red line towards Watford.

_____ 5. I'm at West Harrow Station on the purple line. How do I get to South Harrow?

    a. Change at Rayners Lane, and travel west on the blue line for three stops.

    b. Change at Rayners Lane, take the blue line, travel south, and then get off after one stop.

    c. Change at Eastcote, take the purple line towards Uxbridge, and get off after three stops.

    d. Travel north on the purple line, and get off at the final stop.

24
A Christmas Card 🎧 24

Dear Uncle Frank and Aunt Jean,

Merry Christmas and Happy New Year!

I can't believe that it's already been a year since we celebrated the holidays together. The weather here has been freezing and we already have 40 centimeters of snow on the ground. We plan on snowshoeing out to the forest this afternoon to cut down a tree. Of course the kids can't wait to decorate it! I've been keeping busy in the kitchen baking traditional Christmas treats and volunteering at the local food bank. It's a busy time of year as donations of **canned items come pouring in**. This time of year always brings out the generosity in people. We will deliver boxes of food to families with low incomes around the area a few days before Christmas. We hope you are all well and that you have a peaceful and pleasant holiday Perhaps next year we will be able to fly away from the cold temperature here and spend the holidays with you by the beach!

With love,

Jenny, Paul, and the kids

⌃ snowshoeing

⌃ Christmas treats

Questions

1. What is the purpose of this card?
   a. To invite Uncle Frank and Aunt Jean for a visit.
   b. To see how the weather is where Uncle Frank and Aunt Jean live.
   c. To let Uncle Frank and Aunt Jean know their relatives will be visiting soon.
   d. To wish Uncle Frank and Aunt Jean a happy holiday.

2. Why is it a busy time of year at the food bank?
   a. The food bank is collecting food to give to low-income families.
   b. There is a lot of baking that needs to be done before Christmas.
   c. It takes a long time to shop for gifts for all the families.
   d. There aren't enough volunteers to help out.

3. What does "**canned items come pouring in**" mean in the reading?
   a. Many people are asking for canned food items.
   b. There aren't enough canned items being donated.
   c. Too many people are giving canned items to the food bank.
   d. The food bank is receiving a lot of canned items at the moment.

4. Where do Uncle Frank and Aunt Jean most likely live?
   a. In the same community as Jenny, Paul, and the kids.
   b. In a warm area far away from Jenny, Paul, and the kids.
   c. Next door to Jenny, Paul, and the kids.
   d. In a low-income neighborhood far from Jenny, Paul, and the kids.

5. Why are Jenny, Paul, and the kids going to cut down a tree?
   a. So they can put it in their home as a Christmas tree.
   b. Because they need it for firewood.
   c. They need it to make their snowshoes.
   d. Jenny needs it to finish making her treats.

25 Search Engine— African Penguin

For homework this week we have to write a report

on an endangered species of our choice. So I chose the

African penguin. Did you know that there are penguins

living in Africa? I typed "African penguin" into an

5 Internet search engine, and this is what came up.

African Penguin | Information and Facts

The African penguin is the only penguin species in Africa. It is usually about 58-63 cm
tall and weighs around 2-4 kg . . .
www.penguins.org/africanpenguin

African Penguin Desktop Wallpaper

Have you found the perfect wallpaper from our Animals & Insects gallery? What about
our beautiful African penguin wallpaper?
www.coolwallpaper.com/african-penguin

Wild Animal News | African Penguin Endangered

The number of African penguins in the wild is dropping faster and faster each year. The
main cause of this is heavy fishing in the waters where the African penguin lives . . .
www.wildanimalnews.net/african-penguin-endangered

African Penguin | Green City Zoo

Come and see the beautiful African penguin at Green City Zoo. We have 20 African
penguins on display at the zoo. Opening times for the penguin pool are . . .

www.greencityzoo.org/birds/african-penguin/

>> search engine

Questions

_____1. What is the writer using the Internet for?

    a. To do research for schoolwork.

    b. To record his thoughts and feelings.

    c. To find a perfect pet.

    d. To adopt an endangered animal.

_____2. What does it mean if a species is "**endangered**"?

    a. There are too many of it.

    b. It is dying out.

    c. It is found all around the world.

    d. Its number always stays the same.

_____3. Which of the following is true about the African penguin?

    a. It's one of two penguin species in Africa.

    b. It weighs around 10 kg.

    c. It's about 60 cm tall.

    d. It lives entirely on land.

_____4. Which two websites will the writer most likely use?

    a. www.greencityzoo.org & www.wildanimalnews.net

    b. www.wildanimalnews.net & www.penguins.org

    c. www.penguins.org & www.coolwallpaper.com

    d. www.coolwallpaper.com & www.greencityzoo.org

_____5. What information are you sure to find on www.greencityzoo.org/birds/african-penguin?

    a. The names of all the penguins at Green City Zoo.

    b. How often they feed the penguins at Green City Zoo.

    c. How old the penguins are at Green City Zoo.

    d. When you can see the penguins at Green City Zoo.

26 | Finding the Road to Happiness

Growing up, it can be hard to imagine doing something different. Our parents give us goals, we work hard, and before long we're on the road to success. But does that road always lead to happiness?

5 In my case it did not. I studied law in university and got hired by a big firm right out of school. At 26 years old I had my own office, and it seemed my future was **set in stone**. But something about **it** didn't feel right. I couldn't stop thinking about how my best years

10 were being wasted while I sat there chained to a desk. Practicing law just wasn't for me.

So I did what most wouldn't dare—I walked away from my job, sold my apartment, and started traveling. I had always wanted to see the world, and this was my

15 big chance. I started writing a blog about my adventures through Africa, Asia, and South America. Now I make a living by teaching and writing.

I might not be rich, but I'm successful beyond my wildest dreams.

« adventure

Questions

_____ 1. What is the main point this article is trying to make?

    a. Practicing law can be difficult.

    b. A travel blog can make money.

    c. It's possible to live your dream.

    d. Never quit your job.

_____ 2. Which of the following is true about the writer?

    a. He was fired by his law firm.

    b. He went to school in Africa.

    c. He got a job at 18 years old.

    d. He earns money by teaching.

_____ 3. What is "**it**"?

    a. A university.   **b.** A parent.

    c. A job.   **d.** The writer's goal.

≫ big firm

_____ 4. Which of the following is the writer most likely to believe?

    a. Only you know what's right for your life.

    b. You should always listen to your parents.

    c. Earning money is the most important thing.

    d. Going to university is a waste of time.

_____ 5. What does it mean if something is "**set in stone**"?

    a. It's very old.   **b.** It won't change.

    c. It's cheap.   **d.** It's heavy.

≫ hire

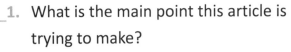

27 🎧(27) Understanding ADHD

Our understanding of Attention Deficit Hyperactivity Disorder (ADHD) has come a long way over the past 10 years. Teachers can now identify the symptoms of a student with ADHD. These symptoms include:

- Trouble paying attention in class.   5
- Losing interest in tasks before they are completed.
- **Putting off** homework and other assignments.
- Trouble organizing schoolwork.
- Forgetting daily tasks like bringing a lunch to school.

After a teacher has identified these   10 symptoms, he or she can help improve the student's classroom experience. Some tips for teachers to remember include:

⌃ hyperactive

⌃ ADHD children lose interest in tasks before they are completed.

⌃ ADHD children have trouble paying attention in class.

64

- Set clear rules for the student.
15 - Offer praise when the student does well.
- Help the student get organized.
- Talk with the student's parents.
- Be patient and understanding.

⌃ Teachers should help ADHD students get organized.

Over 10% of boys and 4.9% of girls in the United States have ADHD.

20 A better understanding of ADHD is very important. It will help us make

sure that these students get the most from their time in school.

Questions

_____ 1. What is this article about?
   a. Teachers.
   b. School tips.
   c. A learning problem.
   d. School assignments.

_____ 2. Which of the following is not a symptom of ADHD?
   a. Losing interest in tasks.
   b. Trouble organizing.
   c. Needing clear rules.
   d. Trouble paying attention.

_____ 3. What does it mean to "**put off**" doing homework?
   a. To give it to someone else.
   b. To avoid doing it.
   c. To have no place to put it.
   d. To do it quickly.

_____ 4. Which of the following is likely true about students with ADHD?
   a. They often have worse marks than other students.
   b. They are often taller than other students.
   c. They are in different classes than other students.
   d. They are better at sports than other students.

_____ 5. Which of the following would likely be a good tip for a teacher with an ADHD student?
   a. Treat the student the same as anyone else.
   b. Let the student do assignments in a quiet room.
   c. Give the student extra homework.
   d. Punish the student when he or she doesn't pay attention.

28 | Never Too Young to Change the World

5 While others were home battling monsters in video games, this American teenager was in a lab battling cancer. His name is Jack Andraka, and he was born in Maryland, United States. At just 15 years old, he was already being described as "the Edison of our times."

It all started when one of Jack's close family friends died from cancer of the pancreas. This type of cancer is particularly dangerous. It has a five-year survival rate of just six out of one hundred patients, and it kills over 10 40,000 people each year.

Jack **didn't take the loss sitting down**. He began to research ways to check a certain protein that is found in pancreatic cancer patients. Jack sent a research plan to 200 teachers at Johns Hopkins University. Only one 15 of **them** replied. Over the following year, Jack spent his free time in the university lab. His hard work paid off. He discovered an early test for pancreatic cancer that will save lives. Not bad for a high school student!

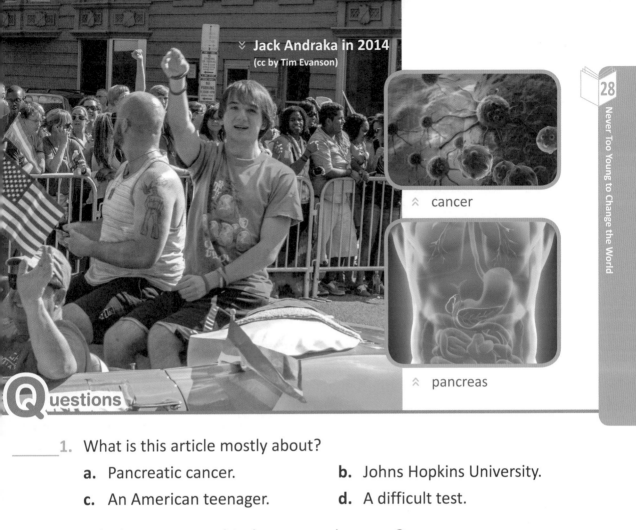

Jack Andraka in 2014
(cc by Tim Evanson)

⌃ cancer

⌃ pancreas

Questions

1. What is this article mostly about?
   a. Pancreatic cancer.
   b. Johns Hopkins University.
   c. An American teenager.
   d. A difficult test.

2. Which event caused Jack to research cancer?
   a. He finished high school.
   b. He got cancer.
   c. A family friend passed away.
   d. He got into Johns Hopkins University.

3. Who does "**them**" mean?
   a. The professors.
   b. Jack's friends.
   c. Jack's family.
   d. Cancer patients.

4. What was Edison most likely famous for doing?
   a. Being a military leader.
   b. Going to high school.
   c. Dying from cancer.
   d. Inventing new things.

5. What does it mean if you "**won't take something sitting down**"?
   a. You're tired and need to sleep.
   b. You will try to solve a problem.
   c. You don't like exercising.
   d. You aren't interested in studying.

29 Gardening in Space

Humans have been growing vegetables down on Earth for ages, so why not try it in space? Well, that's exactly what the crew of the International Space Station is doing far above us.

The experiment is called the Lada Validating Vegetable Production Unit, but to the crew it's the "space garden." The garden is a small space where light and water levels can be controlled, much like a greenhouse. Many different vegetables can be grown in there, including lettuce and peas.

The "space garden" experiment has two main goals. The first is to study the science behind how vegetables are grown in space. This could help future space travel by allowing crews to grow food on their ships. The second goal has to do with how we humans think. Scientists believe that growing our own food helps to **cheer us up**. Therefore, a space garden might make the crew feel more at home, even if it's in deep space.

» The International Space Station

Mizuna lettuce growing in the International Space Station.
(photo from http:// blog.nus.edu.sg/ outofthisworld/)

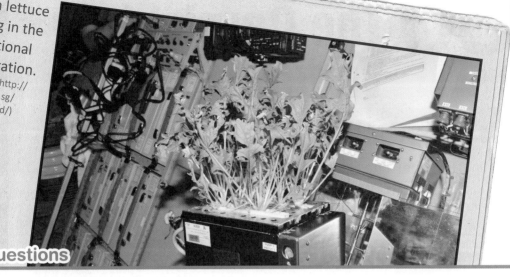

Questions

_____ 1. What is this article about?

    a. A scientist.   **b.** Space.

    c. An experiment.   **d.** Lettuce.

_____ 2. Why was the Lada Validating Vegetable Production Unit built?

    a. To make space travel faster.   **b.** To control light and water levels.

    c. To clean the air.   **d.** To grow food on space ships.

_____ 3. Which of the following is likely true?

    a. People never get homesick in space.

    b. The space garden is a secret experiment.

    c. Fruit cannot be grown in space.

    d. Plants need water and light to grow.

_____ 4. What does it mean to "**cheer someone up**"?

    a. To thank the person.   **b.** To make the person happy.

    c. To listen to the person.   **d.** To make the person gain weight.

_____ 5. What is likely true about the International Space Station?

    a. It was built by many different countries.

    b. It was built to test how humans think.

    c. It does not have a crew.

    d. It is open to everyone.

30 The Carnival of Venice

Come and experience one of the oldest carnivals in Europe! The Carnival of Venice has been held since the 11th century, and now you can see it yourself.

The Carnival will tickle all five of your senses:

- See the beautiful traditional masks which come in all shapes and colors.

- Hear the wonderful music at one of the masked balls held in grand halls throughout the city.

- Taste fine Italian cuisine at one of the Carnival's many feasts.

- Feel the winter air against your skin as you take in shows at St. Mark's Square.

Questions

_____ 1. What is this article about?

    a. A city.   **b.** A feast.   **c.** A mask.   **d.** A festival.

_____ 2. Which of the following is not part of the Carnival of Venice?

    a. Masks.   **b.** Balls.   **c.** Books.   **d.** Feasts.

_____ 3. What does "**kick off**" mean?

    a. To start.   **b.** To play a game.

    c. To go on a trip.   **d.** To dance.

St. Mark's Square

<< The Venetian Carnival is most famous for its distinctive masks. (Wikipedia)

> • Smell the steam rising off your thick, Carnival-style hot chocolate.

15   There's only one way to enjoy these **once-in-a-lifetime** experiences. Book a trip to Venice for next year's Carnival. It usually **kicks off** in mid-February and ends in the first week of March. Book now

20   and join the three million people who attend this world-class event every year!

<< It is common for people to attend the Carnival wearing elaborate costumes, plus masks. (Wikipedia)

_____ **4.** Which of the following is likely true about the Carnival?

    a. It can be hard to book a hotel.

    b. All events are held at St. Mark's Square.

    c. Events are not open to the public.

    d. All food and drink is free.

_____ **5.** Which of the following is a "**once-in-a-lifetime**" experience?

    a. Going to the movies.   **b.** Meeting a movie star.

    c. Buying a new bicycle.   **d.** Watching a football match.

31 Fort Bragg's Glass Beach

The Glass Be
in Fort Bragg
California
(cc by Jef Poskanze)

Fort Bragg's Glass Beach

Welcome to Fort Bragg, California, home of the Glass Beach!
There are three beautiful and unique beaches to visit.

History

⁵ From the early to the late 1960's, citizens of the coastal town of Fort Bragg didn't have a good place to throw away their garbage. Their solution was to throw all their waste over nearby cliffs.

For over half a century, appliances, car parts, bottles, and ¹⁰ other unwanted items were thrown into the ocean. Most of **the garbage was swallowed up by the ocean**, but the glass remained.

Over the years, **Mother Nature turned the broken pieces of glass into smooth sea glass** in many different shapes and colors.

Some of the
rounded gla
the Glass Be
(cc by Jef Poskanze)

Activities

¹⁵ ### Treasure Hunt
Search for different colors of sea glass and see how many you can find. Rare colors are red (from the glass of car lights) and dark ²⁰ blue (from medicine bottles).

Picnic
Enjoy a packed lunch sitting on the rocks and cliffs on Beach #3, the most northern beach.
*Guests are prohibited from taking sea glass from the beach.

1. What is the purpose of this brochure?
   a. To tell people where they can buy beach glass.
   b. To encourage people to visit the Glass Beach.
   c. To let people know where they can throw their garbage.
   d. To tell people about the dangerous rocks and cliffs.

2. Why did the people of Fort Bragg throw their garbage over cliffs?
   a. It was too expensive to throw out in the right way.
   b. They thought that it was good for the environment.
   c. It was the best place to throw out their unwanted items.
   d. They didn't like the beach below the cliffs.

3. What does "the garbage was swallowed up by the ocean" mean in the reading?
   a. People took the garbage from the ocean.
   b. The garbage floated out to sea.
   c. Fish in the ocean ate the garbage.
   d. The garbage disappeared into the water.

4. Why are guests prohibited from taking sea glass from the beach?
   a. They should pay for it before taking it.
   b. People might cut themselves by accident.
   c. If everyone took some there wouldn't be any left.
   d. The glass is much too heavy to carry.

5. What does "Mother Nature turned the broken pieces of glass into smooth sea glass" mean in the reading?
   a. The environment created the sea glass.
   b. How the sea glass was made is unknown.
   c. The women of Fort Bragg made the sea glass.
   d. It was God who created the sea glass.

EMP Museum

I've visited many different museums for my arts column, but none of them was more fun than EMP in downtown Seattle. For one thing, there's the building's unique exterior. How could someone not love the look? There is a train track running through the middle of the building. It looks
5 like a train station on the moon!

It's not only the exterior that **stands out**, but also the exhibits inside. They help to make the EMP Museum truly one of a kind. Most museums focus on the past, but EMP looks at the present. Exhibits cover different aspects of popular culture like music, movies, sports, and even video
10 games. My favorite exhibit was *Seattle Seahawks and the Road to Victory*. **It** really gave me a behind-the-scenes look at Seattle's football team.

Perhaps the EMP Museum is so unique because of the colorful people behind it. It was founded by Microsoft's Paul Allen in 2000, and designed by Frank Gehry, a famous Canadian architect. Just visit EMP and you will
15 see that their hard work has really paid off.

≫ Frank Gehry (1929 —)
(cc by Paul Morigi)

≫ train track going through the
EMP Museum (cc by Reywas92)

≫ EMP Museum looks like a
train station on the moon.
(cc by EMP|SFM)

≫ guitar sculpture in the EMP
Museum (cc by Alex Hendricks)

Questions

_____ 1. What is this article about?

    a. A train station.

    b. An architect.

    c. An exhibit.

    d. A museum.

_____ 2. Which of the following is not true
about EMP?

    a. It has a train track going through it.

    b. It focuses on the present.

    c. It has exhibits on music.

    d. It was designed by Paul Allen.

_____ 3. What does it mean if something "**stands
out**"?

    a. It's waiting in line.

    b. It's hard not to notice.

    c. It's very small.

    d. It's a building.

_____ 4. Which of the following would the writer
not do a column on?

    a. A fine art show .   **b.** A music show.

    c. A football game.   **d.** A new theater.

_____ 5. What is "**it**"?

    a. The EMP exterior.

    b. A movie about Seattle.

    c. The Seahawks exhibit.

    d. The popular culture exhibit.

(33)

33
The Dos and Don'ts of Online Chatting

≫ online
chatting
applications

Whether it's on LINE, Facebook, or WhatsApp, online chatti

is an everyday habit for most of us. But that doesn't mean it's

always safe. Unfortunately, there are some people out there who

will hurt anyone who makes the mistake of trusting them.

5   This doesn't mean we should stop using chat applications. W

should just be careful about **it**.

Here are a few quick tips to help you stay safe:

Questions

_____ 1. What is the main idea of this article?
  a. Chat applications are fun and safe.
  b. Sometimes things look too good to be true.
  c. People often lie about their age online.
  d. Be careful when chatting online.

_____ 2. What is a **"red flag"**?
  a. Something that makes you angry.
  b. Something that makes you careful.
  c. Something that makes you happy.
  d. Something that makes you trusting.

personal information

Don't always trust the people you meet online.

1) Never give personal information to a stranger in a chat. This includes your name, address, and telephone number.

10

2) Do not answer sex-related questions. Any sex-related discussion should be viewed as a **red flag**.

3) Remember that modeling agencies, television shows, and movies don't use chat applications to find new talent. Don't trust anyone saying he or she will find you a job in one of these industries.

15

4) Remember that people can lie about their age online. Someone who says he or she is 16 might really be 40.

5) Don't forget the golden rule: If something looks too good to be true, it probably is.

---

3. Which of the following is not a safety tip from the article?
   a. Never talk about sex.
   b. Never give out personal information.
   c. Never take a job offer.
   d. Never talk about your favorite movies.

4. What is "**it**" in the second paragraph?
   a. Online chatting.
   b. LINE.
   c. A safety tip.
   d. A bad person.

5. Which of the following tips would the writer likely agree with?
   a. Don't chat online after five o'clock p.m.
   b. Don't agree to meet up with online strangers.
   c. Always give a real photo to online strangers.
   d. Always tell online friends your age.

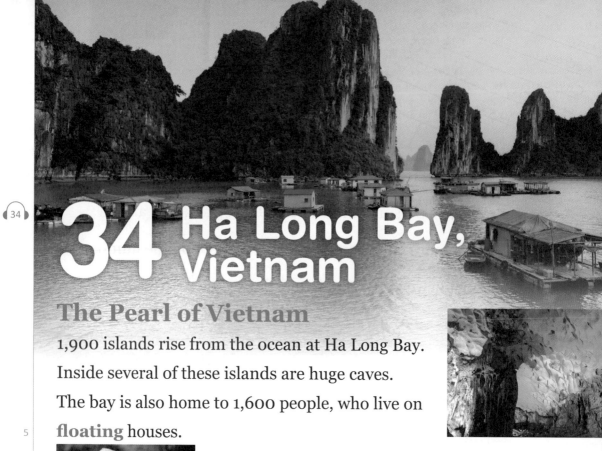

34 Ha Long Bay, Vietnam

The Pearl of Vietnam

1,900 islands rise from the ocean at Ha Long Bay.
Inside several of these islands are huge caves.
The bay is also home to 1,600 people, who live on
floating houses.

"Ha Long Bay was the high point of my trip to Vietnam.
Words can't describe how beautiful it is. You just have to
go there and see it for yourself."   – Andy, London

Questions

1. What's the reading's main message to its readers?
   a. Ha Long Bay has many islands.
   b. There's plenty of nature in Ha Long Bay.
   c. Go and visit Ha Long Bay!
   d. Ha Long Bay is close to Hanoi.

2. I want to go to Ha Long Bay. When's the best time to visit?
   a. Spring and early summer.   b. Fall and early winter.
   c. The end of summer.   d. The end of winter.

3. Which of these describes a "**floating**" house?
   a. It can fly.   b. It's made of stone.
   c. It doesn't sink.   d. It doesn't break.

More than 200 types of fish swim in the
10 clear waters of the bay. And the islands
themselves are home to animals such as
monkeys, lizards, and antelope.
It's no wonder that Ha Long Bay is
regarded as one of the most beautiful
15 bays in the world.

Visiting Ha Long Bay

Ha Long Bay is about four hours by car or bus
from Hanoi. Many travel companies and hotels,
however, offer one- or two-day tours of the bay.
20 These tours usually include transportation,
meals, a guide, and a place to stay the night.
The best time to visit is from March to June.

For more information on Ha Long Bay visit www.halongbay.info

_____ 4. Who is Andy?
  a. Ha Long Bay's official photographer.
  b. A tour guide who works at Ha Long Bay.
  c. A local fisherman.
  d. A traveler who visited Ha Long Bay.

_____ 5. What does the writer mean by describing Ha Long Bay as
  "The Pearl of Vietnam"?
  a. It's the most beautiful place in Vietnam.
  b. It's the hottest place in Vietnam.
  c. It's the hardest place to get to in Vietnam.
  d. It's the most expensive place in Vietnam.

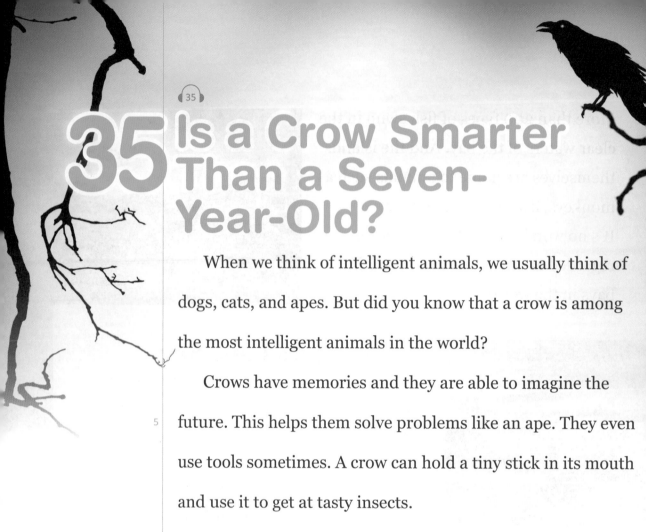

35 Is a Crow Smarter Than a Seven-Year-Old?

When we think of intelligent animals, we usually think of dogs, cats, and apes. But did you know that a crow is among the most intelligent animals in the world?

Crows have memories and they are able to imagine the
5 future. This helps them solve problems like an ape. They even use tools sometimes. A crow can hold a tiny stick in its mouth and use it to get at tasty insects.

It's normal to think a crow in a tree is not **paying any attention** to you. You might be wrong, though. Crows can
10 remember human faces. Some scientists believe that **they** can even tell other crows whether a human is friendly or not.

Some scientists have tested how intelligent crows are

compared to humans. They found that crows were

able to solve a puzzle just as well as a

15 seven-year-old human.

In another test, a crow solved an

eight-stage puzzle within three

minutes.

So if anyone ever calls you "bird brain,"

20 be sure to thank him or her for the compliment.

⌃ Crows use tools sometimes.

Questions

1. What is this article about?

   a. Puzzles.   **b.** Apes.   **c.** Insects.   **d.** Flying animals.

2. Which of the following statements about crows is not true?

   a. They are smarter than adult humans.   **b.** They can use tools.

   c. They can remember human faces.   **d.** They can solve puzzles.

3. What does it mean when a crow "**pays attention**" to you?

   a. It notices you.   **b.** It's scared of you.

   c. It likes you.   **d.** It's angered by you.

4. Which of the following statements is likely true?

   a. Crows can read and write.   **b.** A mask can trick a crow.

   c. Crows can build fires.   **d.** A crow is stronger than a human.

5. What does "**they**" mean?

   a. Scientists.   **b.** Apes.   **c.** Crows.   **d.** Human faces.

36 The Languages of International Business

Most people would agree that English is an important language for international business. There are more speakers of English as a second language than of any other language in the world. However, the idea that English is *the* international business language most likely comes from a Western perspective. 5

Billions of dollars in imports from Asia are bought each year by North American companies. Also, many Western companies now have their own products made in Asia. With Mandarin being the most widely-spoken language in the East, it's possible that it will soon be considered equal in importance to English. 10

company

An increasing number of people are learning Mandarin as a second language. **It has become a huge plus** for those seeking jobs in international business to be able to speak it. Mandarin is a difficult language to learn for many, especially the writing system. Therefore, those who speak 15 Mandarin as a first language may have an advantage over those whose first language is English. However, the people most likely to have successful careers in international business are those with fluency in both languages.

Questions

international business

1. What is this article saying?
   a. English is the most important language to learn.
   b. Speaking Mandarin is more important than speaking English.
   c. Mandarin and English are important international business languages.
   d. Most business around the world is done in Mandarin.

2. Which of the following statements is true?
   a. Most Eastern companies have their products made in North America.
   b. Not many people try to learn how to speak Mandarin.
   c. The English writing system is the easiest writing system to learn.
   d. A large number of people speak English as a second language.

3. What does "It has become a huge plus" mean in the reading?
   a. Being able to speak Mandarin is very difficult for Westerners.
   b. Those who speak Mandarin usually make more money.
   c. For those seeking jobs, being able to speak Mandarin is a big advantage.
   d. These days, most companies ask employees to learn to speak Mandarin.

4. Why might people who speak Mandarin as a first language have an advantage over those with English as a first language?
   a. Learning to write in English is easier than learning to write in Mandarin.
   b. There is more business done in the East than in the West.
   c. More people speak Mandarin as a second language than any other language.
   d. There are more Mandarin speakers in the world than English speakers.

5. What does "an increasing number" mean in the reading?
   a. More and more.
   b. Not as many.
   c. An equal number.
   d. Fewer and fewer.

37

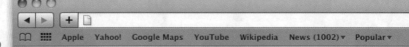

What's Hot and What's Not?

⌃ sunglasses

It's a new year and time for a new style. There is no better time to **bid farewell to last year's looks** than now. You don't want to be caught wearing the same tired styles as you were last year. So, when cleaning out your closet, remember: out with the old and in with the new! 5

Even a girl on a budget can find affordable items by paying attention to sales. Trust me; I know from experience! Many great deals are also available online. You can also check out used clothing stores. The items might not be new, but knee-high boots have been in style for a 10 while. Just take my advice and be careful. Just because something is being sold doesn't mean it's in style!

So, before you make your way to the department store, be sure to check out what's hot and what's not.

What's Hot	What's Not
knee-high boots	ankle boots
gold jewelry	silver jewelry
wool coats	fur coats
oversized sunglasses	cat-eye sunglasses
dark blue jeans	light blue jeans
large purses	small purses

« closet

⌃ knee-high
   boots

⌃ purses

Questions

_____ 1. Which of these statements best describes the main idea of this blog?

   a. It's important to always dress in style.

   b. Everyone should throw away her ugly clothes.

   c. Shoppers should save money by buying items on sale.

   d. Knee-high boots have been in style for a long time.

_____ 2. What is one way shoppers can save money?

   a. By shopping at department stores.

   b. By buying clothes that aren't in style.

   c. By looking for items at used clothing stores.

   d. By selling the clothes they don't want online.

_____ 3. What does "**bid farewell to last season's looks**" mean in the reading?

   a. Sell your old clothes.

   b. Stop wearing last season's clothes.

   c. Throw away clothes from last season.

   d. Give your old clothes to friends.

_____ 4. When was this blog post most likely written?

   a. In January.   b. In December.

   c. In the fall.   d. In the summer.

_____ 5. Who was this blog post most likely written for?

   a. The elderly. b. Women.   c. Men.   d. Everyone.

38 How We View Terrorism

Preface

The following pages will discuss a specific case of terrorism. Therefore I should talk about the concept in general first.

Terrorism is one of the most important issues of our age. It can start wars, bring down governments, and take away lives. But what is terrorism? Giving an answer is difficult, because one person's terrorist could be another person's hero.

If one goes by the dictionary, terrorism is "using violence to scare people for a political goal." This means all wars are acts of terrorism. Because don't all military attacks scare people? Don't **they** all have political goals in mind?

In fact, culture plays a big role in how we view the acts. Many of us see only specific types of attacks by specific groups as terrorism. Those that don't **fit** these ideas aren't called terrorism, even if they should be.

In order to really understand terrorism, cultural influences should be included. We need to ask what makes us think certain ways about terrorism. Keep this question in mind as you continue reading.

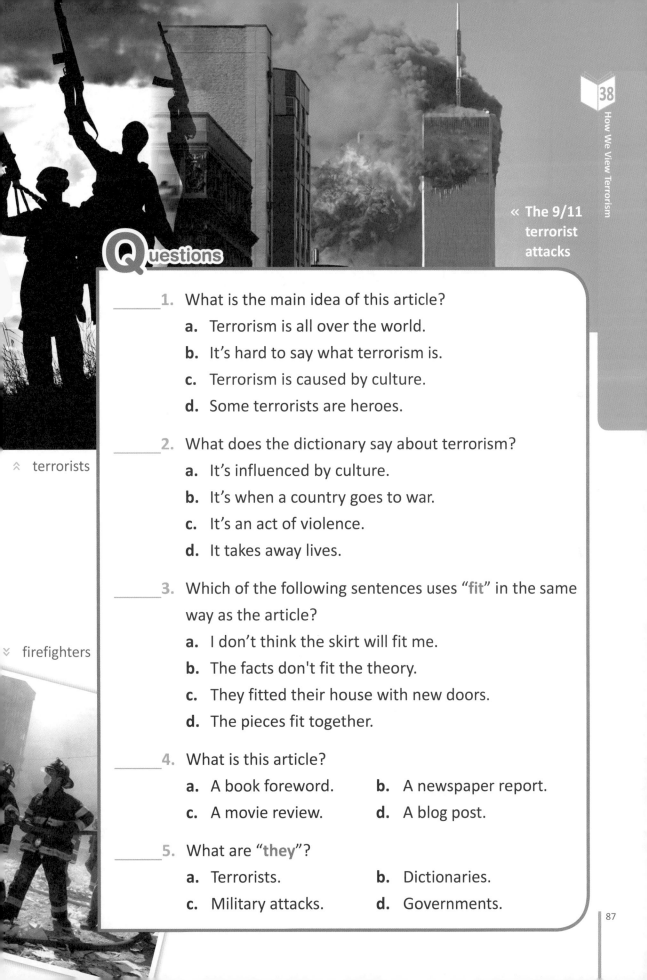

« The 9/11 terrorist attacks

⚐ terrorists

⚐ firefighters

Questions

_____ 1. What is the main idea of this article?
- **a.** Terrorism is all over the world.
- **b.** It's hard to say what terrorism is.
- **c.** Terrorism is caused by culture.
- **d.** Some terrorists are heroes.

_____ 2. What does the dictionary say about terrorism?
- **a.** It's influenced by culture.
- **b.** It's when a country goes to war.
- **c.** It's an act of violence.
- **d.** It takes away lives.

_____ 3. Which of the following sentences uses "**fit**" in the same way as the article?
- **a.** I don't think the skirt will fit me.
- **b.** The facts don't fit the theory.
- **c.** They fitted their house with new doors.
- **d.** The pieces fit together.

_____ 4. What is this article?
- **a.** A book foreword.
- **b.** A newspaper report.
- **c.** A movie review.
- **d.** A blog post.

_____ 5. What are "**they**"?
- **a.** Terrorists.
- **b.** Dictionaries.
- **c.** Military attacks.
- **d.** Governments.

39
Cloud Computing

More and more these days our data is not stored on our computers, USB sticks, or memory cards, but in the cloud. When you store something in the cloud, you basically store it on the Internet. This gives you access to **it** anywhere in the world and saves
5 you a whole lot of space on your own personal devices.

But what are the risks of cloud computing? Recently several famous people had their private pictures stolen from the cloud! If you think about it, though, this is a lot like keeping your money in a bank. As soon as you trust someone else to guard your things, you
10 automatically take on some risk. Banks get robbed, too, but rarely.

There are a couple of things you can do,   » USB stick
though, to lower the risk of a leak. The first: do your homework. Only trust your data to cloud companies that you're sure are able to protect it well. The second: if you really want to keep it
15 secret, **don't put it in the cloud, period.**

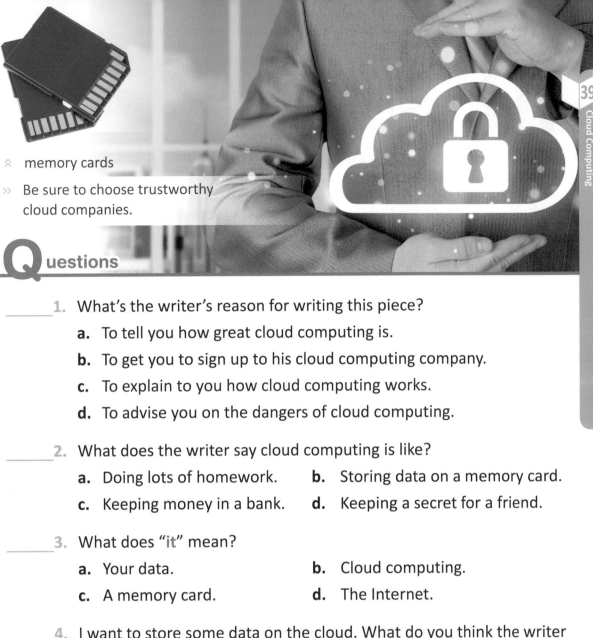

⌃ memory cards

» Be sure to choose trustworthy cloud companies.

Questions

_____ 1. What's the writer's reason for writing this piece?

   a. To tell you how great cloud computing is.

   b. To get you to sign up to his cloud computing company.

   c. To explain to you how cloud computing works.

   d. To advise you on the dangers of cloud computing.

_____ 2. What does the writer say cloud computing is like?

   a. Doing lots of homework.   **b.** Storing data on a memory card.

   c. Keeping money in a bank.   **d.** Keeping a secret for a friend.

_____ 3. What does "**it**" mean?

   a. Your data.   **b.** Cloud computing.

   c. A memory card.   **d.** The Internet.

_____ 4. I want to store some data on the cloud. What do you think the writer would tell me?

   a. It's mostly safe, but be careful.

   b. It's completely unsafe. Keep your things off the cloud.

   c. It's totally safe. Put everything on there.

   d. The cloud? Don't clouds have to do with weather?

_____ 5. What does the writer mean by "**don't put it in the cloud, period**"?

   a. Don't put it in the cloud for too long.

   b. Don't put it in the cloud at all.

   c. Don't put it in the cloud and take it right out again.

   d. Don't put it in the cloud forever.

40 | Iceland

Iceland is a large island in the North Atlantic Ocean. With its long history, friendly locals, and **jaw-dropping** scenery, it's a wonderful place to visit. Here are some cool facts about Iceland:

1. Iceland has about 130 volcanic mountains.

2. Most Icelanders believe in elves—magical beings that live in rocky places and cause trouble if someone bothers them.

3. Most buildings in Iceland use volcanic energy for their heating and hot water.

4. Icelanders drink more Coca-Cola per head than any other nationality in the world.

⌃ Reykjavik, capital of Iceland

5. One of the most popular sports in Iceland is handball, which is like soccer except that you use your hands.

6. In June and July, playing midnight golf is a popular activity, as during these months the sun never sets.

7. Reykjavík is the world's northernmost capital city.

8. Iceland's national dish is *hákarl*—rotten shark meat.

⌃ volcano in Iceland

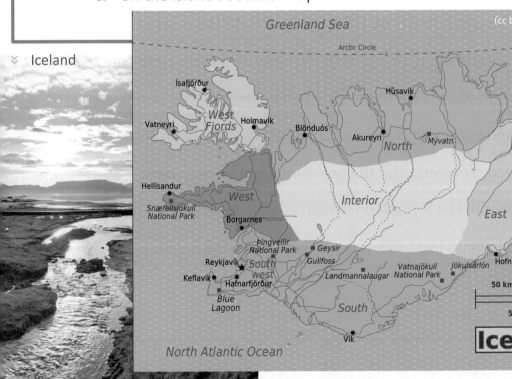

Questions

_____ 1. Which of the following could be the title of this article?
- **a.** Iceland: Land of Green Energy.
- **b.** The History of Iceland.
- **c.** A Visitor's Guide to Iceland.
- **d.** Interesting Iceland.

_____ 2. What do Icelanders do more than anyone else in the world?
- **a.** Play golf.
- **b.** Eat seafood.
- **c.** Drink Coca-Cola.
- **d.** Go hiking.

_____ 3. What does the writer mean when he describes Iceland's scenery as "**jaw-dropping**" ?
- **a.** It is very gray.
- **b.** It will make you go, "Wow!"
- **c.** It is difficult to travel over.
- **d.** It is mostly big cities.

_____ 4. What can you tell by looking at the map of Iceland below?
- **a.** Most of the cities are in the east.
- **b.** The capital city is in the north.
- **c.** Few people live in the center of the island.
- **d.** Most of the national parks are in the West Fjords.

_____ 5. Where is Vik?
- **a.** In the eastern part of the island.
- **b.** On the northwest coast.
- **c.** On the island's southern tip.
- **d.** In the center of the island.

Iceland

From: Amy Mason <k.mason@homepro.com>

To: Jason Porter <porter_jason@fastmail.com>

Date: July 19, 2015 at 4:20 p.m.

Subject: New Listings

Hi Jason,

There are some new listings in your desired neighborhood.

The first home is on Riverside Drive, across from a large park on a

quiet street. It has three bedrooms (two upstairs, one downstairs) and

5 two bathrooms. All appliances are brand new. The roof and windows were

replaced last month and the backyard is private and nicely landscaped.

Unfortunately, this home does not have a garage.

The second home is on Hill Street, close to the overpass. The backyard

requires landscaping (a tree is blocking sunlight from entering the largest

10 bedroom window). There are only two bedrooms (but don't worry; the

unfinished basement could be turned into a third bedroom). The roof and

stove need replacing, and the bathroom and kitchen need

some repairs. **On a positive note**, it has a large garage!

If you would like to view these listings, let me know.

15 Thanks,

Amy

⌃ garage

1. What is the purpose of this email?
   a. To see what neighborhood Jason would like to live in.
   b. To tell Jason about homes he may be interested in buying.
   c. To find out what Jason is looking for in a home.
   d. To let Jason know that he should buy in this neighborhood.

2. What do both of the homes described have in common?
   a. They both have two bathrooms.
   b. They both have garages.
   c. They both need new windows.
   d. They both have backyards.

3. Why did Kelly say "on a positive note" when telling Jason that the second home has a large garage?
   a. To point out that even though the home has lots of problems, it does have one good thing.
   b. To let Jason know that it may be possible to add a large garage to the home.
   c. To make Jason feel happy about choosing this home.
   d. To tell Jason that it will cost him more money in the long run to buy this home.

4. What is Amy's job?
   a. She's a landscaper.   b. She does home repairs.
   c. She sells appliances.   d. She helps people buy homes.

5. Which of the following is most likely important to Jason?
   a. Having a home with three bedrooms.
   b. Finding a home that needs landscaping.
   c. Living close to an overpass.
   d. Making his own repairs to his home.

overpass

42 Crosstalk of the Town

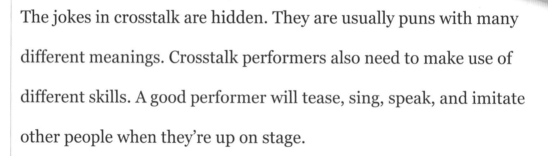

Crosstalk is a Chinese tradition with a long history and a bright future. It involves one or more performers having a conversation full of jokes and

5　funny stories. **This** might sound simple, but it's not. The jokes in crosstalk are hidden. They are usually puns with many different meanings. Crosstalk performers also need to make use of different skills. A good performer will tease, sing, speak, and imitate other people when they're up on stage.

10　Crosstalk has a history stretching back to ancient China, and it shows in some of the subject matter. More traditional performers

« Jiao-Nan Wu is a famous Taiwanese crosstalk performer.
(cc by JeanHavoc)

» crosstalk performers

tend to make fun of how inconvenient life was in the old days.

But not all crosstalk shows focus on the past. The "**new blood**"

performers address modern relationship issues, such as breaking up

15　by email. In China, foreigners are even creating crosstalk shows in

English. One day we might see crosstalk shows all over the world.

Questions

_____1. What is the main idea of this article?
   a. Crosstalk is old, but it's still popular.
   b. Crosstalk started in ancient China.
   c. Foreigners like crosstalk.
   d. Crosstalk uses lots of puns.

_____2. Which of the following is not true about crosstalk?
   a. Performers sometimes sing.
   b. Jokes can be hidden.
   c. It's possible to have just one performer.
   d. Shows only focus on past events.

_____3. What is a "**new blood**" performer?
   a. Someone who is Chinese.　　**b.** Someone who is young.
   c. Someone who tells jokes.　　**d.** Someone who is good at crosstalk.

_____4. Which of the following topics might a traditional crosstalk performer choose?
   a. Writing on Facebook.　　**b.** Getting water from the river.
   c. Eating airplane food.　　**d.** Surfing the Internet.

_____5. What is "**this**"?
   a. Ancient China.　　**b.** A hidden joke.
   c. A crosstalk show.　　**d.** A tradition.

(43)

World Magazine

I just got this month's issue of *World Magazine*!

I can't wait to read it. Let's look at what's inside!

WORLD MAGAZINE   July 2015

CONTENTS

Special Articles

« magazines

Questions

_____ 1. What is the point of the table?
- **a.** To show you who works for the magazine.
- **b.** To show you where you can buy the magazine.
- **c.** To show you what's inside the magazine.
- **d.** To show you who buys the magazine.

_____ 2. Which of the following can you read about in the magazine?
- **a.** A festival in a foreign country.
- **b.** How to apply makeup.
- **c.** This year's most popular video game.
- **d.** New ways to grow plants.

_____ 3. Which of the following is probably true about the article on page 23?
- **a.** It suggests that we should kill more sharks.
- **b.** It suggests that sharks aren't as bad as you think.
- **c.** The writer is someone who hates sharks.
- **d.** It tells you how to cook using shark meat.

_____ 4. I want to read the article about the cure for the common cold. Which page should I turn to?
- **a.** Page 30. **b.** Page 55. **c.** Page 15. **d.** Page 43.

_____ 5. What's on page 2 of the magazine?
- **a.** An article about another planet.
- **b.** An article about traveling in Europe.
- **c.** A quick review of recent events.
- **d.** A message from the magazine's editor.

44

The True Cost of a Tasty Steak

A new study has shone a light on the negative effects of agriculture on our climate. It was conducted by a team of scientists at Bard's College in New York. **They** wanted to find out what foods produced the most carbon, which is the gas behind global warming.

The study singles out cattle farming as being bad for the environment in several different ways. Beef production uses 28 times more land than the production of other meats like chicken and pork. It also produces five times more carbon. The numbers are even more shocking when beef is compared with vegetables. For example, beef production results in 11 times more carbon than potato production.

pork

beef

cattle farming

⌄ steak

The results of the study are being heavily discussed in scientific **circles** around the world. The most important point is the link between climate change and what we eat. Public debate

20 has focused on cars, industry, and airplanes as the biggest causes of global warming. This study will change how people think about the problem.

Questions

1. What is this article about?
   a. The food we eat.
   b. Global warming.
   c. A study.
   d. Cattle farming.

2. Which of the following is not true?
   a. Cattle farming is bad for the environment.
   b. Chicken production uses less land than beef production.
   c. Potato farms produce more carbon than cattle farms.
   d. The study was conducted by Bard's College.

3. Who are "**they**"?
   a. Local food businesses.
   b. Scientists at Bard's College.
   c. Cattle farmers.
   d. The public.

4. What would the writer probably think?
   a. We should eat less meat.
   b. More of us should drive cars.
   c. We should grow our own food.
   d. Carbon doesn't cause global warming.

5. What does "**circle**" mean?
   a. A shape.　**b.** A group.　**c.** A farm.　**d.** A subject.

45 | Malala Yousafzai

⌃ Malala Yousafzai (born July 12 1997) (cc by Russell Watkins/Department for International Development)

In October 2014, 17-year-old Malala Yousafzai was awarded the Nobel Peace Prize. She was the youngest winner of this prize in history. How could this young woman have
5 earned such a big honor?

Malala was raised in the northwest of Pakistan. Her father was an activist who spoke out against the Taliban. **She followed in his footsteps** by also becoming an activist. Malala began to speak out on the equal right of girls to an education.

10 By the time Malala was 15 years old, she was a well-known human rights activist. She appeared in a documentary and wrote a blog about her life under the Taliban army. The Taliban learned about Malala and her activities and made a death threat against her. One day on her way home from school, she was shot in the face.

15 Luckily she survived. Even though she was terribly hurt, Malala did not let this experience stop her. Today, she continues to speak out about women's rights and education for all. **It is no wonder she was awarded this honorable prize**.

Barack Obama meets with Malala Yousafzai in 2013.

Questions

_____ 1. What is the purpose of this reading?

    a. To tell readers about human rights activities.

    b. To teach readers about life in Pakistan.

    c. To explain why Malala Yousafzai won a Nobel Peace Prize.

    d. To help readers understand the Taliban.

_____ 2. What happened after Malala was shot?

    a. She started writing a blog about the Taliban.

    b. She stopped speaking out about equal rights.

    c. She left Pakistan with her father.

    d. She kept on working as an activist.

_____ 3. What does "**She followed in his footsteps**" mean in the reading?

    a. Malala wrote a blog like her father.

    b. Malala did the same thing as her father.

    c. Malala was being protected by her father.

    d. Malala's father taught her about the Taliban.

⌃ International Poetry Festival 2013, to honor Yousafzai

(cc by Tubeth2000)

_____ 4. Why did the Taliban want to kill Malala?

    a. Because she won the Nobel Peace Prize.

    b. Because she was speaking out about equal rights.

    c. Because she made death threats against them.

    d. Because she wanted to leave Pakistan.

_____ 5. What does "**It's no wonder Malala was awarded this honorable prize**" mean in the reading?

    a. It's doesn't make sense that she won the prize.

    b. It's only fair that she won the prize.

    c. It's not a surprise that she won the prize.

    d. It's great news that she won the prize.

« Yousafzai's portrait at the Nobel Peace Center (cc by Jeblad)

46 Blueberries: The Superfood!

Have you ever heard of superfoods? They're foods that are especially good for your body, and eating them will help keep you healthy. There are lots of superfoods out there: broccoli, green tea, strawberries, and many types of fish, **to name but a few**. My favorite superfood, though, is blueberries. They're a great source of fiber and vitamin C. And they're really low in fat and sodium (that's salt), so they won't damage your heart. Check out the nutritional information about blueberries in the table on the right.

⌄ broccoli

5

Questions

_____ 1. Why is the writer interested in blueberries?
- **a.** They taste delicious.
- **b.** They're good for your health.
- **c.** You can bake them into a pie.
- **d.** They have a beautiful color.

_____ 2. Which of the following is not true about blueberries?
- **a.** They're low in fat.
- **b.** They're high in fiber.
- **c.** They contain a lot of salt.
- **d.** They're good for your heart.

_____ 3. What does the writer mean when he uses the phrase "**to name but a few**" after listing some superfoods?
- **a.** Superfoods are hard to find.
- **b.** He could give many more examples.
- **c.** He can't think of any more superfoods.
- **d.** Superfoods have difficult names.

Nutrition Facts: Blueberries

Serving Size 100 grams

Amount Per Serving

Calories 57

Calories from Fat 3

%Daily Value*

Total Fat 0.3 g		
Saturated Fat 0 g	1%	
Sodium 1 mg	0%	
Total Carbohydrate 14 g	0%	
Fiber 2 g	5%	
Protein 1 g	10%	
Vitamin A 1%	1%	
Calcium 1%	Vitamin C 16%	
	Iron 2%	

* "Daily value" is the total amount of something that a healthy body needs each day. The label lists vitamin C at 16% daily value. That means that one serving of blueberries provides 16% of the vitamin C you need each day.

4. I'm having some blueberries as an afternoon snack. If I eat 200 grams of blueberries, how many calories will I take in?

   a. Fifty-seven.

   b. Twenty-three.

   c. Two hundred seven.

   d. One hundred fourteen.

5. I just ate 100 grams of blueberries. How much of the total amount of fiber I need per day did I get?

   a. 10%   b. 5%   c. 16%   d. 2%

47 A Note for the House-Sitter

(47)

Cindy,

While we are away . . .

- The plants on the front porch need watering twice a we

- Garbage pick-up is at 7 a.m. on Tuesdays.

  5   Items for recycling won't be picked up while we are gone

- Feed and walk Barney twice a day. He really likes to
  chase the pigeons in the park.

  Make sure he always has at least a liter of water in his
  bowl.

  10 - The air conditioner is set at 26 degrees. Please do not
  lower the temperature as we are trying to keep our
  electric bills low.

≪ feed

Questions

_____ 1. Why did the Smiths leave this note?
- **a.** To tell Cindy how to take care of the garbage.
- **b.** To tell Cindy how to take care of their child.
- **c.** To tell Cindy how to take care of their home.
- **d.** To tell Cindy how to take care of their plants.

_____ 2. Why isn't Barney allowed in the basement?
- **a.** He is afraid of cockroaches.
- **b.** The temperature is too low.
- **c.** It's too dark down there.
- **d.** He might eat poison.

<< front porch

⌃ air conditioner

- Be certain you don't forget to set the security alarm before you go to sleep. The code is 5389.
- We have a problem with cockroaches. John has set
5 traps for them in the basement, so please don't let Barney go down there (they are filled with poison).

We really appreciate your looking after things while we are gone. We trust that we are leaving our home and precious Barney in capable

20 hands.

Mr. and Mrs. Smith

⌃ microwave

P.S. We left your payment by the microwave.

_____3. What does "**in capable hands**" mean in the reading?

   a. With a responsible person.   **b.** With a helpful neighbour.

   c. With a kind friend.   **d.** With an intelligent teenager.

_____4. Who wrote the note?

   a. Mr. and Mrs. Smith.   **b.** The house sitter.

   c. Mr. Smith.   **d.** Mrs. Smith.

_____5. Who is Barney?

   a. Mr. and Mrs. Smith's son.   **b.** Mr. and Mrs. Smith's daughter.

   c. Mr. and Mrs. Smith's bird.   **d.** Mr. and Mrs. Smith's dog.

48 Little Taipei

↑ minced pork rice

Review—
Little Taipei

By Jeremy Cook

Little Taipei is a small, newly opened restaurant in downtown East City. Don't be fooled by the plain whitewashed walls and cold metal tables and chairs. The food here is warm, exciting, and very, very delicious.

Opened by Gary Lin last October, Little Taipei is East City's first
5　restaurant serving real Taiwanese food.

Dishes like minced pork rice, Taiwanese meatballs, the oyster omelet, and the very popular *xiaolongbao* (steamed soup dumplings) are packed full of taste and character.

You won't find all of Taiwan's famous dishes here, however.

Questions

_____ 1.　What is the writer doing in the article?
　　a. Saying what he loves about Taiwanese food.
　　b. Saying what he thinks about a Taiwanese restaurant.
　　c. Teaching people how to cook Taiwanese dishes.
　　d. Giving people tips on how to open a Taiwanese restaurant.

_____ 2.　Why doesn't Little Taipei serve stinky tofu?
　　a. The owner doesn't like the taste of that dish.
　　b. Tofu is too expensive to buy.
　　c. The owner doesn't think locals would enjoy it.
　　d. It was so popular that it's all sold out.

⌃ Taiwanese meatballs ⌃ oyster omelet ⌃ xiaolongbao (steamed soup dumplings) ⌃ stinky tofu

10 "We felt that some dishes, like stinky tofu and chicken feet, would just be too strange for most locals," Lin says. "We wanted to give people **a taste of Taiwan**, but felt it was important to have dishes that we knew local people would enjoy."

Lin also serves Taiwan's unique bubble milk

15 tea—sweet milk tea with "bubbles" of chewy tapioca.

Finally, a special tip from this writer: for dessert, order the mango shaved ice. It's out of this world!

» bubble milk tea

» chewy tapioca

3. What does the owner mean when he says he wanted to give people "a taste of Taiwan"?
   a. He wanted to let people sample Taiwan's delicious food.
   b. He wanted to make dishes only Taiwanese would enjoy.
   c. He only wanted to use cooks who were born in Taiwan.
   d. He wanted to mix Taiwanese and American cooking styles.

4. Which of these do you think the writer does not like about the restaurant?
   a. The food.   b. The service.   c. The location.   d. The appearance.

5. What score do you think the writer would give the restaurant?
   a. 9/10   b. 5/10   c. 2/10   d. 4/10

49 Taiwan Blue Magpie

Taiwan is a great place for birdwatching. **It** is home to over 600 species of birds, some of which aren't found anywhere else in the world! One of these is the Taiwan blue magpie. Here's the data on the Taiwan blue magpie

5 from my bird guide. If you want to look up other birds, the index will tell you where in the book to find them.

TAIWAN BLUE MAGPIE
Urocissa caerulea

Length: 64–69 cm   Wing size: 18–21 cm   Tail length: 40 cm

Where: Taiwan only; common.

Habitat: Low mountains (100–1,200 m); forests and forest edge.

Appearance:

Almost entirely deep blue. Head black. Wings blue with white tips. Tail long with black and white tips to each feather. Underparts light blue. Beak red. Eyes yellow.

Voice: Like a cruel laugh—*kyak-kyak-kyak-kyak*.

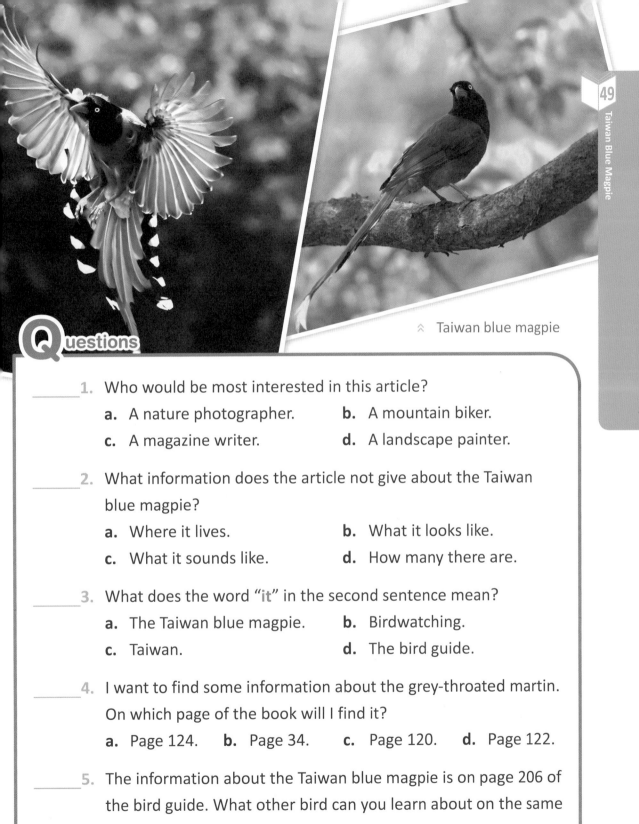

⌃ Taiwan blue magpie

Questions

_____ **1.** Who would be most interested in this article?

    a. A nature photographer.   **b.** A mountain biker.

    c. A magazine writer.   **d.** A landscape painter.

_____ **2.** What information does the article not give about the Taiwan blue magpie?

    a. Where it lives.   **b.** What it looks like.

    c. What it sounds like.   **d.** How many there are.

_____ **3.** What does the word "it" in the second sentence mean?

    a. The Taiwan blue magpie.   **b.** Birdwatching.

    c. Taiwan.   **d.** The bird guide.

_____ **4.** I want to find some information about the grey-throated martin. On which page of the book will I find it?

    a. Page 124.   **b.** Page 34.   **c.** Page 120.   **d.** Page 122.

_____ **5.** The information about the Taiwan blue magpie is on page 206 of the bird guide. What other bird can you learn about on the same page?

    a. The red-billed blue magpie.   **b.** The azure-winged magpie.

    c. The Eurasian magpie.   **d.** The common magpie.

50 Watch Out! Your Smartphone Can Make You Go Blind

A Canadian teenager recently lost her sight after several hours of watching Netflix on her smartphone, and is still not quite back to 20/20 vision after three months of wearing corrective eyeglasses. It may be rare for such **symptoms** to last so long. Doctors say, however, that the number of cases of poor vision is increasing rapidly, especially among young gadget-users. What was once mainly a health issue of the aged is now becoming common even among the very young as they spend ever more of their time looking at tiny screens.

The problem, doctors say, is that small print and pictures viewed up close force the eye's muscle to bend more than it should in order to focus. This tires the muscle, often resulting in partial loss of vision by the end of the day.

Happily, common sense is enough to avoid serious eye damage from smartphones. Spending less time on your favorite gadget, and letting your eyes rest before using it again, should make for a safe experience online. So give your eyes a break!

⌄ Give your eyes a break!   5

10

⌃ Smartphones cause sight problems.   15

Questions

1. What is the main idea of this article?
   a. Canadians spend too much time on their smartphones.
   b. People's eyesight gets weaker as they get older.
   c. Watching a small screen for a long time can hurt your eyes.
   d. Eye doctors don't want people to use smartphones.

2. How does using smartphones cause poor eyesight?
   a. By making people's eye muscles bend too much.
   b. By making people want to watch TV all the time.
   c. By making people stop listening to eye doctors.
   d. By making people stay at home for several hours.

3. What does the word "symptoms" mean in the article?
   a. Having a smartphone.   b. Watching a lot of TV.
   c. Wearing special eyeglasses.   d. Losing your sight.

4. What is suggested in the article?
   a. Strong light is the main cause of vision loss in young people.
   b. Vision loss is only a problem for people over 50.
   c. You should wear glasses when looking at your smartphone.
   d. Looking at smartphone screens is very bad for people's eyes.

5. What advice does the writer give teenagers to avoid serious eye damage?
   a. To stop using computers forever.
   b. To spend less time on their smartphones.
   c. To talk to an eye doctor.
   d. To play with their friends more.

TRANSLATION

1 世上最倒楣的人

我一定是世上最倒楣的人。從這學期開始，我坐在茉莉旁邊整整一個月的時間，每天我都有機會跟她說說話，我會請教她問題，或是跟她借支筆，雖然她的回應不多，但這樣讓我能夠看到她那迷人的笑容。

沒錯，眨眼間一切都變了。吉米上課時太聒噪，所以老師要我們交換位子。就這樣，他坐到前排，而我則被困在後排。

我以為這樣也沒關係，我只要靜心等待就好。本來打算在暑假之前，請茉莉加我為臉書好友，但是她在放假前的最後一週都缺席。

她到底去哪裡了？我還是不確定，我只知道今年的暑假一定會很漫長。

2 從台灣捎來的明信片

親愛的貝琪：

台灣比我想像中更酷，台灣人十分友善，風景秀麗，而且甜點好吃得不得了。

妳還記得我之前對於騎腳踏車有多緊張嗎？我的擔心真是多餘的，很多人會騎著腳踏車繞台灣一圈，他們稱此活動為「環島」，也就是「環繞島嶼」的意思。這裡沿途也都有很棒的設施場所，可以輕易地找到修車店或買杯咖啡喝，妳喜歡的話，還可以在寺廟過夜喔。

我目前最喜歡台灣的一點是便利商店，我想這一定是全世界最方便的國家，幾乎每個轉角都有一家便利商店，而且都會賣這種小小的三角飯糰，騎了一天漫長的路途後，這真的是很棒的點心。

我知道妳本來應該與我同在，無奈事與願違。但是別擔心，我明年會再陪妳回來環島一次！

妳的好友
琳達

3 校園舞會

　　春假即將到來，我們學校打算辦場慶祝春假的迪斯可舞會，我真的很期待。我的朋友比利會和他的樂團一起演出，他們真的很不賴。還有某些學長會擔任播放音樂的 DJ，但我聽說丹尼・馬龍的音樂品味很差勁。我還聽說肯尼・瓦力斯也會參加舞會。他好可愛！不曉得他會不會邀我共舞……但有點不好意思的是，我必須跟媽媽拿舞會門票的費用，因為我上週末把所有的零用錢都花在從購物中心買的那件新上衣……真是糟糕！

4 形容「瘋癲」的成語

鮑伯：你在唸什麼書？

約翰：英文成語的起源和意義，我在準備考試。

鮑伯：喔！這我拿手，考考我。

約翰：形容某人 head in the clouds 是什麼意思？

鮑伯：意思是脖子特別長，像長頸鹿一樣。

約翰：差遠了。意思是不切實際，就像你以為潔西卡會和你出去一樣。

鮑伯：取笑我很好玩是吧！再考我一句。

約翰：raining cats and dogs 是什麼意思？

鮑伯：這簡單，意思是下傾盆大雨。

約翰：但你知道這句成語的起源嗎？

鮑伯：不知道耶。

約翰：雖然有不同說法，不過有人說是因為從前的水災都會沖刷出貓和狗的屍體。

鮑伯：好噁心。現在換我考你：你知道 mad as a hatter 是什麼意思嗎？

約翰：你考倒我了。

鮑伯：意思是你瘋了，起源來自於帽子都是以危險化學物品製作的年代。

約翰：完全符合我唸這些成語的心境啊！

我下週即將前往德國度假，雖然曾在學校學點德文，但很多都忘了，所以我行前必須複習一下。我用的是英德片語書，內含豐富的實用片語。第一頁的內容如下：

交際類

基本單字與片語	打招呼
是。	哈囉！
不是。	早安！
不好意思。	午安！
謝謝你！	晚安！
對不起！	再見！

人際互動

你叫什麼名字？	你會說英文嗎？
我叫做……	我不懂你的意思。
你好嗎？	可以再說一次嗎？
我很好，謝謝， 你呢？	請說慢一點。

詢問地點

……在哪裡？

銀行	城堡	博物館
書局	醫院	郵局
公車站	飯店	火車站

6 **喝水的時機**

大家都知道喝水有益健康，很多人已經依照建議一天喝八杯水（2000 cc）。但是你知道喝水的時機很重要嗎？以下列出喝水的最佳時刻：

- **剛起床：**早上喝兩杯水，能活化內臟與淨化血液。
- **飯前：**飯前30分鐘喝杯水，能帶來兩大好處，一方面能避免過度飲食，另一方面則可幫助身體吸收食物的養分。
- **洗澡前：**洗澡前喝杯水能降低血壓。
- **運動前後：**運動時，重點在於為身體補充足夠的水分，而且能有益肝臟。
- **睡前：**睡前喝杯水，能改善心臟的健康狀態。

7 你最喜歡哪一堂課？

克里斯 今天的數學課有夠枯燥乏味。

約翰 哈哈哈，不是所有的科目都有點無趣嗎？

克里斯 才不是！有的課很棒，我就很期待英文課，因為能讓我看懂喜歡的節目。

約翰 我想我有時也蠻喜歡上歷史課。

克里斯 你喜歡歷史課的哪些方面？

約翰 我喜歡思考還沒有智慧型手機、電腦甚至是電視的年代是什麼樣子。一百年前的生活真是截然不同。

克里斯 是啊，那時無聊多了。

約翰 哈哈哈，那你最喜歡哪一堂課呢？英文？

克里斯 不好說，但我也許會選科學課，現代電子設備的運作方式讓我十分著迷。我們小的時候，電腦可是好大一台，現在 iPad 平板電腦卻可薄如紙張，我喜歡了解促成這些現象的科技。

8 來自家鄉的問候

　　親愛的辛蒂，我只是想告訴妳，我們全家都好以妳為榮。妳出國留學似乎只是昨天的事，但真不敢相信已經四年了。恭喜妳畢業，我們都好想妳，米特恩也是喔。我給了牠一根大骨頭來共襄盛舉。

　　我問老爸我們是不是能去見證妳的大日子，他說旅費會太貴。不過還好妳過幾個月就回家啦！

　　別忘了帶禮物回來囉，老媽說德國的甘貝熊軟糖最好吃了。

　　還記得之前妳告訴我妳想當科學家，那已經差不多是十年前的事了，現在的妳等於美夢成真。妳一定要託人幫妳拍幾張畢業典禮的照片，記得秀出妳那燦爛的笑容。最重要的是：好好享受備受矚目的那一刻，因為妳實至名歸！

115

9 做自己勝過追求完美

不用事事追求完美並無妨。

聽起來很怪，不是嗎？這是因為我們已慣於追求完美：父母要求我們考試滿分；我們希望晉升人生勝利組；我們的腦子永遠轉個不停，精益求精讓自己更上一層樓。

不過，注意囉。有目標固然是好事，但「做自己」有可能讓你更容易達成目標。完美主義只會增加困難度，也就是讓你過度思考每件事，徒增壓力和拖垮你的腳步。最好是冷靜地從容不迫完成每件事，即使出了差池，你也能學到經驗而不再犯錯。

切記，完美二字的定義甚至不存在，這不過是自我陶醉的一種想法。即使你真的達到了「完美境界」，你也不會發現，因為你的心思還是會過度忙於如何改善這種完美現況。

10 歡迎來到日麗狗狗公園！

為了確保您盡興遊玩狗狗公園，請詳讀以下規定。

- 請於進入公園前，取下愛犬的領圈。護欄容易卡住領圈，使狗狗受傷或窒息。

- 請幫愛犬收拾善後。我們希望狗狗公園能保持狗狗與飼主皆開心遊玩的乾淨狀態！

- 進入狗狗公園前，記得讓愛犬善加運動。雖然此公園是讓狗狗消耗體力的絕佳去處，但是精力過於旺盛的狗狗可能會引起麻煩！

- 記得讓小型愛犬待在小型犬區。與大狗一起玩耍的小狗經常因而受傷！

- 請勿帶著孩子進入狗狗公園。許多大狗會於公園內四處奔跑，可能會對小孩造成危險。

- 未取得飼主同意之前，請勿餵食其他人的愛犬。有的狗狗患有食物過敏症，隨意餵食十分危險。

- 愛犬生病時，請勿進入公園，否則可能傳染其他狗狗。

希望您和愛犬都能享受快樂時光

11 最美味的爭論：誰發明了漢堡

馬克：我們旅途的最後一站還去造訪了漢堡的發源地。

克勞斯：等一下，漢堡的發源地是德國。

馬克：我想你誤會了，漢堡是美國發明的，我們在家鄉常說：「漢堡就像是你聽到蘋果派就會想到美國人的意思一樣。」要證明這件事的話，很簡單，看看麥當勞就知道了。

克勞斯：胡扯！每一個德國人都知道漢堡來自漢堡市，光看單字的拼法就是證據。

女服務生：不好意思兩位先生，我不小心聽到你們爭論的內容，我算是個老饕，也剛好熟悉漢堡的二三事，其實某種程度上來說，你們兩位的論點都對。漢堡肉排的部分是來自德國，但漢堡麵包的部分則是美國人發明的。多加了漢堡麵包的原因，是因為工廠工人必須快點吃完「漢堡肉排」，才能繼續回到工作崗位。

克勞斯：所以肉排是最重要的部分。

馬克：什麼！漢堡麵包才是製成漢堡的靈魂。

女服務生：老天啊……

12 奧林匹克運動會獎牌排行榜

　　我是運動迷，所以理所當然，我會非常期待下一次的奧運。我來自大不列顛，雖然我們贏得的獎牌一直不算最多，但成績也算夠好了。獎牌排行榜裡幾乎總是大獲全勝的國家就是美國。

　　事實上，以夏季奧運會而言，美國贏得的金牌與總獎牌數最多。看到了嗎？他們是下頁表中的第一名。自現代奧林匹克運動會於1896年創辦開始，美國已贏得2552面獎牌，包括1018面金牌，連我都不得不承認這是一件很了不起的事。

117

你會有談戀愛的機會嗎？

你上輩子是什麼人？你何時會有小孩？

他／她對你的好感超越友情嗎？你會找到心靈伴侶嗎？

如果你對自己的過去、現在或未來有任何疑問，
讓克萊拉夫人來為你解惑

「我認識克萊拉夫人之前，很擔心自己永遠結不了婚。但她告訴我未來一年內就會結婚，現在我終於不再擔心，也以正面的態度看待自己的未來！」

史蒂芬妮，34歲

「我一直很喜歡研讀生物學而不知道原因。克萊拉夫人告訴我，因為我前世是一名科學家！」

潔西卡，25歲

「克萊拉夫人告訴我，我無法升遷的原因在於缺乏自信。現在我已經是大公司的副理。」

大衛，42歲

「我一直很擔心考試會考不好。克萊拉夫人告訴我，只要我有唸書，就會通過考試……我真的考過了！」

史丹，16歲

馬上撥打電話給克萊拉夫人！
897 - 432 - 9890

14 機器人是幫手？還是取代人類的工作地位？

　　上百年來，人類一直夢想著機器人能代勞我們的事務。然而，現在夢想即將成真了，這一切卻可能變調為一場噩夢。

　　理論上，這樣的概念可行：也就是機器人執行所有事務，讓我們有更多休憩的時間。但實務上卻截然不同，當機器人取代人類勞工，人類就等於失業，根本沒有時間悠閒放鬆心情，而是必須瘋狂另覓高就。況且，你還得找到一份無法被機器人取代的工作。

　　人類勞工未來將被大規模地取而代之。一項研究結果顯示，至2030年，美國將有45％的工作由機器人任職。也許不久的將來，機器人就能擔任護理師、教師、店員、清潔工，甚至是作家。事實上，電腦早已接管某些新聞內容的撰寫職務。

　　很有可能連這篇文章都是機器人所寫的喔！

15 神奇麥斯

神奇麥斯

牠大名鼎鼎，
聲名遠播人類圈與狗界；
牠大名鼎鼎，
身為寵物還懂得為正義挺身而出。
麥斯！大家輕聲呼喊，你逮不到牠。
牠一天能刨挖五個花圃；
麥斯！大家流傳著，牠快如疾風，
勢必讓郵差付出代價。
有人試著接受，有人無法理解，
一隻狗狗為何能夠異軍崛起。

他們問，
一隻綁在院子裡的跳蚤狗，
為何能如此神通廣大。
只要問問在動物收容所工作的老人，
是他發現麥斯的空狗籠；
或是問問麥斯幫助過馬路的那位盲婦，
麥斯想要的報酬不過是摸摸肚子。
麥斯！大家說牠真是了不起，
我希望牠能停下腳步安頓下來；
麥斯！大家說牠是活生生的見證，
證明狗狗也有走路有風的時候。

16 全球最多觀光客的城市

有著「愛之都」別稱的巴黎，是一個充滿生活樂趣的城市。巴黎是羅浮宮的所在地，擁有史上最棒的藝術品館藏。還有世上最知名的景點之一：艾菲爾鐵塔。此外，稱霸全球的超讚餐廳與服飾店同樣現身於巴黎。

這樣的城市，充滿古色古香的教堂、別緻咖啡廳、迷人的小巷弄街道以及美侖美奐的建築物；這樣的城市，充斥著畫家、詩人、哲學家與老饕。不過巴黎最令人矚目的大概是觀光之都的身份！2014年，超過1500萬人來此一遊，使巴黎成為全球觀光客排行第三多的城市。

事實上，還有許多城市呈現觀光客人數超越本地人的現象，尤其是旅遊旺季的時候。請參閱下表了解全球最受歡迎的城市排行榜。

為了準備考試而苦讀，確實令人倍感壓力。無論你準備多麼充分，考試當天都有可能出差錯。也許是題目出其不意，或是你亂了陣腳而寫錯答案。

幸好有許多方法能確保杜絕上述情況，只要謹慎且運用系統化的方式來準備考試即可。以下是一些幫助你成功準備考試的重要訣竅：

- 練習考古題，讓自己熟悉學科主題。
- 與同學組讀書會，了解大家的意見。
- 攝取有助記憶的食物，例如魚肉、水果和堅果。
- 運用視覺工具來唸書，例如圖表與圖片。
- 不用總是在同一個場所唸書。
- 在整潔安靜的環境唸書。
- 不時小憩，讓腦筋休息一下。
- 規劃好考試當天的動線流程，避免到校途中出現突發狀況。

18 七色土

問： 七色土？那是什麼？

答： 七色土是模里西斯小島上的一個特殊景點。

問： 這個景點有何特別之處？

答： 那裡的土壤和多數棕色或黑色土壤不同，它是彩色的！

問： 哇！有哪些顏色呢？

答： 紅色、咖啡色、紫羅蘭色、綠色、藍色、紫色和黃色。

問： 這些顏色難道不會混在一起？要如何分辨各種顏色？

答： 奇妙的地方就在這，每種顏色都自成一格，形成美麗的漩渦與色塊圖案。
非常賞心悅目！

問： 什麼原因造成此現象呢？

答： 你知道嗎？沒人能解答！此外，七色土永遠不會被沖刷殆盡，即便這區的降雨量非常豐沛，很奇怪對吧？

問： 那麼我可以去觀光嗎？還是那裡禁止進入？

答： 你可以去觀光。事實上，七色土是模里西斯最熱門的觀光景點之一。
在日出的時候抵達那裡，可以看到七色土最鮮豔分明的景象。

問： 該如何抵達七色土？

答： 距離首都路易斯港約一小時的車程。你也可以參加觀光巴士行程，
當地有許多這類服務！

19 無國界醫生日記

親愛的日記：

　　我一直嚮往加入無國界醫生的團體，因為我想助人。這個團體的成員會前往任何需要醫護資源的國家，無關政治，一切以患者的就醫需求為主。身為醫生，等於擁有造福他人的醫術，因此我決定與此團體並肩作戰。

　　想當初，我以為我是會去幫阿爾巴尼亞或某些非洲小村莊的兒童打針，完全不曉得自己會到「災區」前線。我們已經在賴比瑞亞駐紮一年的時間，看來也終於戰勝了伊波拉病毒，但我仍需遵守規定，進入醫院前，我必須穿戴四層塑膠防護衣。防護衣十分悶熱，但我絕不能碰觸到自己的臉部，否則等於讓自己陷入險境。

　　這裡聚集了世界各地的醫生和護理師，我們大家都有一個共識：那就是這份苦差事，總得有人扛下來。

20 電影預算明細表

　　拍電影是一件斥資的事。史上拍攝成本最高的電影（2011年的《神鬼奇航四：幽靈海》）花費超過3.78億美金。電影公司通常對於拍片費用以及花費項目十分保密，所以我們不太能確切知道電影特效或音樂方面等的開銷有多少。保守來說，每部電影依其性質而花費不等。

　　每部電影都不同，有些是以太空場面或大量驚人怪物為主題的大製作科幻片，可能會將絕大多數的預算放在特效；而劇情片等其他類型的電影，預算就會低一點，而且是著重在演員片酬方面，而非特效。大家可參考布魯斯威利所主演的電影《驚心動魄》的預算明細表，該片總預算為74,243,106元。

21 台灣樹王

賴倍元有「台灣樹王」之稱，30多年前，他離開經營有成的貨運家族事業，開始在台中大雪山購買大面積的土地並種植樹木，數量竟超過25萬棵！

但是，賴先生為什麼決定以超過20億台幣的金額來購地種樹？他說，以往他工作時所服務的客戶，都是汙染地球的企業，他覺得自己必須有所行動，來恢復地球的生機。

賴先生所種植的樹木均可生長一千年以上！此類樹木能穩固土壤，有助於水土保持。

部分樹木可生產要價高昂的木材，但賴先生的原則是，絕不容許任何人砍伐他的樹木，儘管他可從中獲利不少。

只要樹王還在的一天，他的樹林就會安然無恙。

22 分手非易事

吉兒‧布朗是熱門電視節目的主持人，她今天的專訪對象，
是剛出新書的兩性專家莎拉‧湯普森。

吉兒： 可否請您介紹一下新書內容？

莎拉： 新書主題是我個人認為非常重要的課題：分手。

吉兒： 很多人都曾有這樣的經驗，可否請您再詳細說明一下？

莎拉： 本書一針見血地說明和情人分手的感覺：天底下沒有比這更難受的事。你會猜忌自己，懷疑自己是否還能再談戀愛，還會喪失自信，彷彿世界末日到來。

吉兒： 分手的人要如何度過這難熬的情傷時期？

莎拉： 切記，這些感受都是暫時的。雖然現在令人痛苦萬分，但時間會沖淡傷痛。過了一兩年，你將會以全新的視野回顧這段分手過往。因此，重點在於別再傷害自己或任何人。

吉兒： 說得真好，真希望當年我還是青少女的時候，妳的書已經出版了。

23 搭捷運

　　地鐵（亦稱捷運系統或地下鐵路）堪稱現代都市的重要建設，上百萬名通勤族每天都靠平價的地鐵迅速通往目的地。

　　目前全球營運中的地鐵系統超過160處，規模最大的捷運系統非「上海地鐵」莫屬，路線總長將近550公里。不過，站點最多的地鐵系統，則由紐約市地鐵奪冠，竟然有421個停靠站！

　　只要使用捷運地圖，就能了解捷運系統的動線，所有路線均以顏色區分，且列出各站的標示與名稱。你會發現某些站點有兩條路線交集經過，也就是所謂的「轉運站」，利用轉運站，你可以不用離開捷運系統，直接轉乘另一個路線。

　　以下列出典型的捷運地圖範本。你覺得自己會使用捷運地圖穿梭於都市嗎？

24 聖誕卡片

親愛的法蘭克叔叔和珍阿姨：

聖誕快樂及新年快樂！

　　真不敢相信距離我們上次一起過節已經一年了。這邊的氣候超冷，積雪已經40公分深。我們打算今天下午穿上踏雪板，前往森林砍樹，孩子們當然迫不及待想要好好裝飾聖誕樹！我一直在廚房忙著烘烤傳統的聖誕點心，還到當地的食物銀行當志工。這是一年之中最忙碌的時候，因為會湧進各地捐贈的大量罐頭食品。這個時節總是能讓大家慷慨解囊響應活動，我們會在聖誕節前幾天，將裝箱的食物送往本區的低收入戶。希望你們一切都好，度過平和愉快的假期。或許明年我們能遠離這裡的低溫氣候，和你們一起在海灘享受美好的假期！

愛你們的珍妮、保羅和孩子們

我們本週的作業，是必須自己選一種瀕臨絕種的動物來寫報告，所以我選非洲企鵝。你知道非洲也有企鵝嗎？我在網路的搜尋引擎輸入「非洲企鵝」後，就出現這樣的搜尋結果。

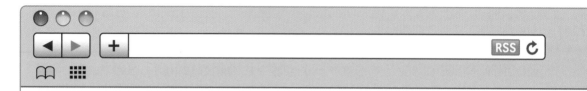

非洲企鵝｜資訊與事實

非洲企鵝是唯一在非洲繁殖的企鵝，一般約 58—63 公分高，體重約 2—4 公斤重……

www.penguins.org/africanpenguin

非洲企鵝桌布

在我們的動物和昆蟲圖庫裡找到最佳桌布了嗎？何不參考我們美輪美奐的非洲企鵝桌布？

www.coolwallpaper.com/african-penguin

野生動物新聞｜瀕臨絕種的非洲企鵝

野生非洲企鵝的數量每年都在急速減少，主要成因在於非洲企鵝所居住的水域魚類遭到濫捕……

www.wildanimalnews.net/african-penguins-endangered

非洲企鵝｜綠城動物園

來綠城動物園觀賞絕美的非洲企鵝，目前園區中展示二十隻，企鵝區的開放時間為……

www.greencityzoo.org/birds/african-penguin

26 尋覓幸福之道

成長過程中，有時難以想像我們能夠實現不同作為。父母給我們努力的目標，我們努力實現，不用多久時間，我們已踏上成功之路。但是這樣的方向，一定會帶來幸福嗎？

我就是個反例。大學時期主修法律，畢業後立即受聘於一家知名事務所。26歲時，我已經擁有自己的辦公室，未來看似已然成形，但我總是覺得不對勁。我無法擺脫自己的巔峰時期就要這樣被綁在辦公桌前的想法，律師這個職業就是不適合我。

所以我大膽做了多數人不敢做的決定──離職、賣掉公寓，然後開始旅行。我一直很想出去看看世界，這是個大好機會。我把前往非洲、亞洲與南美的冒險旅程寫在部落格，現在的我以教書和寫作維生。

也許我不富有，但以這樣瘋狂的夢想而言，我已經超越自己的成就。

27 了解「注意力不足過動症」

過去十年來，我們對「注意力不足過動症」（ADHD）的了解已越來越深入，現今的教師已可確認學生是否患有ADHD，其症狀如下：

- 上課無法專心。
- 還沒完成某事物，就失去興趣。
- 功課作業方面會拖拖拉拉。
- 學業方面的組織統整能力有障礙。
- 容易忘記日常例行事務，例如帶午餐去學校。

當教師確認出上述症狀時，即可協助改善該名學生的課堂體驗。教師可參考的訣竅包括：

- 為此類學生清楚制定規矩。
- 當此類學生表現良好時，需給予讚美。
- 協助此類學生學習組織統整的能力。
- 與此類學生的家長促膝長談。
- 以耐心和體諒的心境教導此類學生。

美國有超過10％的男孩與4.9％的女孩患有ADHD，善加了解ADHD十分重要，才能讓我們確保此類學生在校得到最佳的學習效果。

28 改變世界永遠不嫌早

當其他人在家埋首於電玩打怪時，有位美國青少年卻已在實驗室裡對抗癌症，他叫做傑克·安卓卡，生於美國的馬里蘭州。當傑克年僅15歲時，就已享譽「現代愛迪生」的盛名。

一切始於傑克的某位世交好友死於胰臟癌，這種癌症格外危險，只有6％的患者可熬過五年的存活率，每年的死亡人數超過四萬人。

此憾事激起了傑克的鬥志，他開始研究能夠檢查胰臟癌患者體內某種特定蛋白的方法。他將研究計畫傳給約翰霍普金斯大學的200名教師，卻只有一位教師回覆。接下來的一年，傑克將所有閒暇時間投入大學實驗室，他的心血總算開花結果，他發現了能夠在早期檢測到胰臟癌的方法，進而拯救生命。以一名高中生的成就而言，還真是不簡單！

29 太空園藝

人類自古以來，都在地球上種植蔬菜，在外太空如法炮製有何不可呢？而國際太空站的組員，就在那遙遠的太空著手進行這樣的計畫。

這項實驗稱為「拉達驗證蔬菜生產裝置」，不過對組員來說，其實就是個「太空花園」。此花園是一個狹小空間，加以控管照明與灌溉程度，類似溫室的概念，可種植許多不同蔬菜，包括萵苣和豌豆。

「太空花園」實驗有兩大目標。第一，研究蔬菜於太空生長的狀態，可協助往後前往太空的宇航員，於太空船自行種植食物；第二，在於了解我們人類的思考模式。科學家認為，自行種植食物具有療癒心情的效果，因此，太空花園也許能讓遠赴外太空的宇航員更有家的感覺。

30 威尼斯嘉年華會

歡迎前來體驗歐洲最古老的嘉年華會之一！威尼斯嘉年華創始時間可追溯至 11 世紀，現在你也能親眼見證。

威尼斯嘉年華將滿足你五種感官的體驗：

* 看見形形色色的華麗傳統面具。
* 在威尼斯市各大宴會廳舉辦的化裝舞會聽見美妙的音樂。
* 在嘉年華的眾多饗宴之中，品嚐義大利料理。
* 在聖馬可廣場欣賞表演節目時，感受冷颼颼的冬季寒風。
* 嗅聞具有嘉年華風味的濃醇熱巧克力所散發的熱氣。

想擁有畢生難得的體驗只有一個辦法，那就是預定前往威尼斯的行程，參加明年的嘉年華會。嘉年華通常於二月中旬開始，並於三月的第一週結束。馬上訂票，參加這場每年均有三百萬人共襄盛舉的世界級盛典！

31 布拉格堡的玻璃海灘

布拉格堡的玻璃海灘

歡迎來到擁有玻璃海灘的加州布拉格堡！這裡共有值得一訪的三大壯麗獨特海灘。

歷史起源

1960 年代初期至晚期之間，布拉格堡的沿岸居民苦無棄置垃圾之處。因此，他們的辦法就是將所有廢棄物丟至鄰近的懸崖。

超過半世紀以來，家電、汽車零件、瓶瓶罐罐以及其他廢棄物，不斷被擲入大海。而大海就這麼照單全收多數垃圾，只有玻璃留在原地。

多年來，大自然將破碎的玻璃片，沖刷為擁有各種不同形狀與色澤的圓滑海玻璃。

觀光活動

尋寶遊戲	野餐
尋找不同色彩的海玻璃，看看能找到幾種顏色。罕見的顏色為紅色（汽車燈所殘留）以及深藍色（藥瓶所殘留）。	可於最北邊的 3 號海灘，坐在岩岸崖邊享受野餐。 *遊客禁止帶走海灘上的海玻璃。

32 EMP博物館

　　我為了藝術專欄造訪過各式各樣的博物館，但沒有一所博物館如西雅圖市中心的EMP如此耐人尋味。其中一項原因包括博物館建物擁有獨特外觀，誰會不喜愛這樣的建築？而且火車軌道還穿越博物館中央，彷彿月球上的火車站！

　　不是只有外觀獨樹一格，館內展覽更使EMP博物館成為一絕。多數博物館將重點放在過去，但EMP卻著重於現代潮流，展覽內容涵蓋不同流行文化，例如音樂、電影、運動，甚至是電玩。我最喜歡的展覽是《西雅圖海鷹隊的必勝之路》，讓我得以一窺西雅圖美式足球隊的幕後秘辛。

　　或許EMP博物館的獨到之處，在於有趣的創辦人。此博物館由微軟的保羅・艾倫於2000年所創，並由知名的加拿大建築師法蘭克・蓋瑞所設計。只要一遊EMP，你就會理解他們的心血造成多大的迴響。

33 線上聊天的準則與禁忌

　　無論是使用LINE、臉書或WhatsApp，線上聊天彷彿是多數人的日常習慣，但卻不見得安全。不幸的是，某些有心人會利用別人不小心上當而傷害對方。

　　不過，我們不需因此停用聊天應用軟體，只要小心為上即可。以下列出幾個保護自己的速成訣竅：

1 與陌生人聊天時，切忌提供個人資訊，包括真實姓名、地址或電話號碼。

2 切勿回答與「性」相關的問題，應將任何性話題視為禁區。

3 切記，模特兒經紀公司、電視節目和電影不會使用聊天應用軟體來徵選新秀。切勿相信自稱願意幫你在此類產業謀得一職的人。

4 切記，大家都可以在網路世界謊報年齡，自稱16歲的男性或女性，真實年齡可能是40歲。

5 千萬記住黃金法則：如有任何好康讚到令人難以置信，通常不是真的。

34 越南下龍灣

越南之珠

下龍灣的海面上散佈1900座島嶼，許多島嶼裡還藏有偌大的洞穴。下龍灣亦為1600名水上人家的家園。

「下龍灣是我至越南旅遊最棒的景點，美不勝收的景象無法言喻，一定要親眼見證才能體會。」

—來自倫敦的安迪

清澈的海水裡悠游超過200種的魚類，島嶼本身更是猴子、蜥蜴與羚羊等動物的棲息地，難怪下龍灣號稱世上最美的海灣之一。

前往下龍灣觀光

下龍灣距離河內大約四小時的車程（開車或坐巴士），不過許多旅行社和飯店提供一或兩天的海灣行程，此類觀光行程通常包含交通工具、食宿和導遊服務，而最佳的觀光時節為三月至六月。

如需了解下龍灣的更多資訊，請至 www.halongbay.info。

35 烏鴉比七歲小孩聰明嗎？

論及聰明的動物，我們通常會想到狗狗、貓咪和猩猩。但你知道烏鴉才是世上最聰明的動物嗎？

烏鴉的記性好，還能預想事物的後續發展，這樣的能力可幫助他們如猩猩般解決問題。有時甚至還會使用工具，烏鴉可用喙嘴叼住細棍，藉此捕捉美味的昆蟲。

大家常認為樹上的烏鴉不會注意我們的一舉一動，不過，這麼想可能是錯的。烏鴉能記得人類的臉孔，部分科學家認為烏鴉甚至會通知同類某人友善與否。

某些科學家以人類的標準來測試烏鴉的聰明程度，他們發現到，烏鴉解謎的的能力等同七歲小孩。在另一項測試中，烏鴉竟然在三分鐘內解開了八階段的謎題。

所以，如果以後有任何人叫你「禽腦」，記得謝謝他們的讚美。

36 國際商業語言

多數人應該都認同，英語為重要的國際商業語言。和其他語言相較下，英語是全世界最多人說的第二語言。然而，認為英語是國際商業語言的看法，多出自西方國家的角度。

北美的公司每年都自亞洲進口數十億元的商品。此外，現有許多西方國家的公司產品都於亞洲製造。在東方世界最盛行中文的情況下，中文的重要程度可能很快就會和英文並駕齊驅。

越來越多人將中文當作第二語言，對於尋求國際商業職務的人來說，會說中文等於是一大加分。對許多人而言，中文實屬難學的語言，尤其是書寫方式，因此，中文為母語的人，可能比英文是母語的人還佔優勢。不過，能在國際商業領域成功駕馭事業的人，通常都能流利運用這兩種語言。

37 時髦與過時

　　新的一年意味新造型的到來，現在正是向去年的穿著打扮說掰掰的大好時機。你一定不想被發現自己身穿去年流行的過時衣著，所以，整理衣櫃的時候，記得汰舊換新！

　　即使是預算有限的女生，也能透過留意特價消息的方式找到平價單品，請相信我的經驗之談！網站上也有許多很棒的促銷活動，還可以到二手衣店挖寶，或許非全新商品，但及膝馬靴類的商品一直都不退流行。不過，我想提醒大家小心，上架銷售的商品不見得符合流行趨勢！

　　因此，在你前往百貨公司之前，記得先了解一下時髦與過時的衣著重點。

時髦商品	過時商品
及膝馬靴	踝靴
金飾	銀飾
羊毛大衣	皮草大衣
大鏡框墨鏡	貓眼造型墨鏡
深藍色牛仔褲	淺藍色牛仔褲
大包包	小包包

38 我們對恐怖主義的觀感

前言

　　以下內容將討論特定的恐怖主義例子，因此我想先大致討論一下恐怖主義的概念。

　　恐怖主義在我們的年代可說是最重要的議題之一，它能發動戰爭、擊潰政府和奪取性命。但何謂恐怖主義？我們難以提出具體的答案，因為某人眼中的恐怖份子，有可能是其他人眼中的英雄。

　　翻閱字典即可發現，恐怖主義的定義為「基於政治目的而使用暴力嚇阻他人」。這表示所有的戰爭皆為一種恐怖主義的形式，因為所有的軍事攻擊不都具有嚇阻效果嗎？不都是以政治為目的嗎？

　　事實上，文化在此類行動扮演著重要角色。很多人僅視發動特定攻擊類型的特定族群為恐怖份子，而不符此觀點的族群行為則不被冠上這樣的頭銜，儘管這些行為應納入恐怖主義的範圍。

　　為了真正了解恐怖主義，我們應考量文化的影響力，也就是捫心自問，是什麼因素使我們對恐怖主義產生既定印象。請於之後閱讀本書的過程中，一邊謹記此問題。

39 雲端運算技術

越來越多的電子資料現今已不再儲存於電腦、隨身碟和記憶卡，而是存放於雲端。將資料置於雲端的做法，基本上等於儲存於「網路」，無論身在何處，我們都能存取資料，節省個人電子裝置的不少空間。

但是雲端運算技術有何風險？近來不少名人存放於雲端的私人照片紛紛遭竊！想想看，這種情況與在銀行存錢十分相似，當你信任他人保管自己的身外之物，就必須承擔某種程度的風險，因為銀行也會遭搶，只是較為罕見罷了。

不過，你可以採取某些措施來降低風險。首先：做好功課，只信任能夠妥善防護資料的雲端公司。再者，如果你真的希望保密，那就不要將任何東西存放於雲端，就是這麼簡單。

40 冰島

冰島是一座位於北大西洋的碩大島嶼。悠久歷史、親切的本地人以及令人不可置信的美景，絕對是值得一訪的超棒景點。以下是關於冰島的二三事：

1 冰島擁有130座火山。

2 多數冰島人均相信精靈的存在，也就是居住於岩穴等處、具有魔法的生物，如果他們受到打擾就會製造麻煩。

3 冰島的多數建物均採用火山地熱能源來供應暖氣與熱水。

4 冰島人所喝下的可口可樂，比世上任何一個國家還多。

5 冰島最熱門的運動之一就是手球，玩法類似足球，差別在於用手。

6 六月和七月所流行的活動就是夜間高爾夫，因為這是屬於永晝的兩個月份。

7 雷克雅維克是全球地理位置最北邊的首都。

8 冰島的道地食物是 hákarl，意即腐臭鯊魚肉。

寄件人：艾咪・梅森 <k.mason@homepro.com>

收件人：傑森・波特 <porter_jason@fastmail.com>

日期：2015年7月19日下午4點20分

主旨：新物件

嗨，傑森：

你喜歡的社區釋出了一些新物件。

第一間房子位於河岸道，在一座位於僻靜街道上的大型公園對面。共有三房（樓上兩房，樓下一房）兩衛，所有的家電設備皆為全新，上個月才換過屋頂和窗戶，而且附有優美造景的私人後院，可惜的是這間房子沒有車庫。

第二間房子則位於希爾街，靠近高架橋的地方。後院需要造景整理（有棵樹會擋到陽光，導致最大間的臥室沒有採光）。只有兩房（但別擔心，未裝修的地下室可改造為第三間房間），屋頂和爐具均需更換，浴室和廚房也需要整修。好消息是附有一間大車庫！

如果你想參觀這些物件，再和我聯絡。

謝謝

艾咪

42 家喻戶曉的相聲藝術

　　「相聲」是擁有悠久歷史與大好前景的一項中國傳統。呈現方式是由一或多名表演者，聊一些笑話和詼諧有趣的故事。聽起來或許簡單，其實不然。相聲以隱喻的方式帶出笑點，通常皆為一語雙關的內容，相聲表演者亦需運用不同技巧，優秀的表演者上台表演時，能呈現說學逗唱的絕活。

　　相聲的歷史可追溯至中國古代，相聲主題也會略為著墨這樣的過去。越來越多的傳統表演者，開始喜歡拿古人不便的生活來開玩笑，但並非所有的相聲表演均著重於過往。「新一代」的表演者則以現代人的感情關係為主題，例如用電子郵件分手，居住在中國的外國人甚至發想英文的相聲表演。也許有朝一日，我們能在世界各地看到相聲藝術。

我剛拿到這個月新出的《世界雜誌》！真是令人迫不及待，來翻閱一下有什麼內容吧！

世界雜誌

2015年七月刊

目錄

美味牛排背後的真正代價

　　近來的新研究開始著眼於農業對氣候帶來的負面影響，這項研究是由紐約巴德學院的科學團隊所進行，他們希望了解何種食物會產生最多碳氣，也就是造成全球暖化的元兇。

　　該研究直指養牛業對環境帶來眾多層面的不良影響。生產牛肉所畜牧的土地面積，比生產雞肉或豬肉所需的土地面積多28倍，亦產生高出5倍的碳氣。與蔬食相較下，數據更是驚人，例如生產牛肉所釋放的碳氣，比生產馬鈴薯多11倍。

　　全球科學界皆熱烈討論此研究結果，最重要的觀點在於氣候變遷與食物之間的關聯。過去大眾爭辯的論點均認為汽車、工業以及飛機是造成全球暖化的主因，但是本研究將讓人們對此問題改觀。

---

45 **瑪拉拉・優薩福札伊**

　　2014年10月，17歲的瑪拉拉・優薩福札伊獲頒諾貝爾和平獎，她成為史上最年輕的和平獎得主。這樣一位年輕女性，何以榮獲此項殊榮？

　　瑪拉拉成長於巴基斯坦的西北部，他的父親是挺身而出抵抗塔利班政權的社運人士，她繼承父親的衣缽，也成為一名社運人士，瑪拉拉開始替女孩爭取受教育的平等權益。

　　瑪拉拉15歲時，已是家喻戶曉的人權捍衛分子。她在紀錄片中現身說法，於部落格寫下受到塔利班軍隊壓迫的生活。塔利班得知瑪拉拉與其主張的行動後，還威脅要置她於死地，她於某日放學回家的途中，因而臉部中槍。

　　她倖存下來，即使受到重傷，仍未因此畏懼而停宕自己的腳步。如今，她仍以女權與全民教育為主題而四處演講，難怪她能獲得此尊榮獎項。

46 堪稱超級食物的藍莓！

你聽過超級食物嗎？此類食物格外有益人體，攝取之後有助維持健康狀態。超級食物族繁不及備載，包括綠花椰菜、綠茶、草莓與各種魚類等等。不過我最喜愛的超級食物就是藍莓，它擁有豐富的膳食纖維和維他命C，而且低脂低鈉（也就是鹽分），因此不會損害心臟。請看看右表所列的藍莓營養成分。

營養成分：藍莓

份量為 100 克
每份所含營養

熱量 57 卡	來自脂肪的熱量為 3 卡

	每日攝取量之百分比 *
總脂肪 0.3 克	1%
飽和脂肪 0 克	0%
鈉 1 毫克	0%
總碳水化合物 14 克	5%
膳食纖維 2 克	10%
蛋白質 1 克	1%
維他命 A 1%	**維他命 C** 16%
鈣 1%	**鐵** 2%

*「每日攝取量」意指健康人體每日所需的營養總量。此表標示維他命 C 的每日攝取量為 16%，意指一份藍莓能提供人體每日所需維他命 C 總量的 16%。

辛蒂：

我們不在的時候……

- 門廊上的盆栽必須一星期澆水兩次。

- 垃圾車會在每週二的早上7點來收垃圾。但我們不在的時候，他們不會帶走需要資源回收的垃圾。

- 記得讓巴尼每天吃兩餐，還有每天遛他兩次。他真的很喜歡在公園追著鴿子跑。確保他的碗裡至少盛滿一公升的水。

- 冷氣已設為20度，請勿調低溫度，因為我們想避免增加電費。

- 確保睡前設好保全警鈴，密碼是5389。

- 我們家有蟑螂肆虐的問題，約翰已經在地下室設好捕蟑陷阱，千萬不能讓巴尼進去（因為四處都是殺蟑藥）。

真的很感謝妳在我們離家時幫忙看家，我們相信妳是照顧我們家和寶貝巴尼的最佳人選。

史密斯先生與太太

註：我們將妳的薪水放在微波爐旁。

48 小台北

評價──

小台北

作者 傑瑞米、庫克

「小台北」是東城市區新開張的一家小餐館，別被它素色白牆與冷調的金屬桌椅唬弄，這裡的食物可是令人感到溫暖、期待且十分可口。

小台北是林蓋瑞於去年十月開店，東城第一家擁有道地台灣料理的餐廳。

肉燥飯、肉圓、蚵仔煎以及超受歡迎的小籠包（也就是蒸湯包），皆充滿風味特色。

不過，這裡並未供應台灣所有的知名小吃。

林老闆表示：「我們覺得像臭豆腐或雞腳等小吃，可能會使本地人望之卻步。雖然我們希望讓大家品嚐看看台灣味，但重點在於當地民眾能享受到合他們胃口的菜色。」

林老闆還有賣台灣獨一無二的珍珠奶茶，也就是香甜的奶茶裡，加入狀如珍珠般的Q彈樹薯球。

最後，作者特別推薦：甜點的部分一定要吃芒果剉冰，簡直是人間美味！

　　台灣是個賞鳥的絕佳去處，超過600種鳥類棲息寶島，有些品種甚至是台灣獨有！其中一種就是台灣藍鵲。我的鳥類百科裡列出的台灣藍鵲資料如下。如果想查詢其他鳥類，此索引提供了書中對應的頁碼供查詢。

台灣藍鵲

學名 Urocissa caerulea

身長：64−69公分　翼長：18−21公分　尾長：40公分

分佈地：台灣特有；普遍。

棲息處：低海拔山區（100−1200公尺）；森林和森林邊緣。

外觀：

幾乎全身呈深藍色。頭部為黑色，藍色的雙翼尾端呈白色。長長尾巴的羽毛尾端則黑白交錯。腹部呈淺藍色。喙嘴為紅色，眼珠為黃色。

叫聲：類似狂笑──嘎嘎嘎嘎

50 小心！智慧型手機會讓你失明

　　近期有名加拿大青少年，以智慧型手機觀看網路串流電視平台Netfilx節目數小時後失明，配戴矯正眼鏡三個月後，仍尚未恢復至1.0的正常視力，這種症狀維持這麼久的情況，算是罕見。不過，醫生說，視力不良的病例迅速增加中，尤其是使用電子裝置的年輕族群。本為長者才會面臨的健康問題，現在卻常見於極低年齡層，因為他們花越來越多的時間盯著小螢幕。

　　醫生說，問題在於近看小字體和圖片，會迫使眼球肌肉為了達到聚焦目的而過度彎曲，導致眼球肌肉疲勞，最後造成喪失部分視力的問題。

　　幸好，只需常識即可避免智慧型手機對眼睛帶來嚴重的損傷。減少使用你喜愛的電子裝置的時間，再次使用之前記得閉目養神片刻，上網就會較為安心。所以，一定要讓靈魂之窗休息一下！

In·Focus 英語閱讀
活用五大關鍵技巧 2

發行人	黃朝萍
作者	Zachary Fillingham / Owain Mckimm / Shara Dupuis
譯者	劉嘉珮
審訂	Richard Luhrs
編輯	丁宥暄
企畫編輯	葉俞均
封面設計	林書玉
內頁設計	鄭秀芳／林書玉（中譯解答）
圖片	shutterstock
製程管理	洪巧玲
出版者	寂天文化事業股份有限公司
電話	02 - 2365 - 9739
傳真	02 - 2365 - 9835
網址	www.icosmos.com.tw
讀者服務	onlineservice@icosmos.com.tw
出版日期	2024年6月 初版再刷
	（寂天雲隨身聽APP版）(0103)
郵撥帳號	1998620 - 0 寂天文化事業股份有限公司

訂書金額未滿1000元，請外加運費100元。
〔若有破損，請寄回更換，謝謝〕

國家圖書館出版品預行編目資料

In Focus英語閱讀2：活用五大關鍵技巧 (寂天雲隨身聽
APP版)/ Zachary Fillingham, Owain Mckimm, Shara
Dupuis 著；劉嘉珮譯. -- 初版. --
[臺北市]：寂天文化, 2021.04 印刷 -
冊；　公分
ISBN 978 - 626 - 300 - 000 - 1(16K平裝)

1.英語 2.讀本

805.18   110004448

ANSWERS

1	**1.** a	**2.** b	**3.** c	**4.** b	**5.** b
2	**1.** c	**2.** c	**3.** b	**4.** b	**5.** b
3	**1.** d	**2.** c	**3.** a	**4.** c	**5.** a
4	**1.** d	**2.** d	**3.** a	**4.** a	**5.** c
5	**1.** c	**2.** a	**3.** b	**4.** b	**5.** d

6	**1.** b	**2.** c	**3.** b	**4.** c	**5.** c
7	**1.** c	**2.** c	**3.** b	**4.** d	**5.** a
8	**1.** b	**2.** d	**3.** a	**4.** c	**5.** c
9	**1.** c	**2.** d	**3.** d	**4.** a	**5.** b
10	**1.** c	**2.** d	**3.** c	**4.** a	**5.** b

11	**1.** c	**2.** b	**3.** a	**4.** b	**5.** d
12	**1.** a	**2.** c	**3.** b	**4.** d	**5.** b
13	**1.** a	**2.** c	**3.** d	**4.** d	**5.** c
14	**1.** b	**2.** b	**3.** a	**4.** d	**5.** b
15	**1.** c	**2.** d	**3.** a	**4.** b	**5.** a

16	**1.** b	**2.** c	**3.** a	**4.** c	**5.** d
17	**1.** a	**2.** d	**3.** a	**4.** c	**5.** a
18	**1.** c	**2.** b	**3.** d	**4.** c	**5.** b
19	**1.** a	**2.** c	**3.** d	**4.** b	**5.** b
20	**1.** c	**2.** a	**3.** c	**4.** a	**5.** d

21	**1.** b	**2.** a	**3.** a	**4.** d	**5.** c
22	**1.** a	**2.** c	**3.** b	**4.** b	**5.** d
23	**1.** a	**2.** d	**3.** c	**4.** a	**5.** b
24	**1.** d	**2.** a	**3.** d	**4.** b	**5.** a
25	**1.** a	**2.** b	**3.** c	**4.** b	**5.** d

26	1. c	2. d	3. c	4. a	5. b
27	1. c	2. c	3. b	4. a	5. b
28	1. c	2. c	3. a	4. d	5. b
29	1. c	2. d	3. d	4. b	5. a
30	1. d	2. c	3. a	4. a	5. b

31	1. b	2. c	3. d	4. c	5. a
32	1. d	2. d	3. b	4. c	5. c
33	1. d	2. b	3. d	4. a	5. b
34	1. c	2. a	3. c	4. d	5. a
35	1. d	2. a	3. a	4. b	5. c

36	1. c	2. d	3. c	4. a	5. a
37	1. a	2. c	3. b	4. a	5. b
38	1. b	2. c	3. b	4. a	5. c
39	1. d	2. c	3. a	4. a	5. b
40	1. d	2. c	3. b	4. c	5. c

41	1. b	2. d	3. a	4. d	5. a
42	1. a	2. d	3. b	4. b	5. c
43	1. c	2. a	3. b	4. d	5. c
44	1. c	2. c	3. b	4. a	5. b
45	1. c	2. d	3. b	4. b	5. c

46	1. b	2. c	3. b	4. d	5. a
47	1. c	2. d	3. a	4. d	5. d
48	1. b	2. c	3. a	4. d	5. a
49	1. a	2. d	3. c	4. c	5. c
50	1. c	2. a	3. d	4. d	5. b